"You want to buy Ladera by the Sea?"

It seemed to take him a moment to even remember that was the name of her family's inn.

"The state does," he corrected her.

Her father, Andy knew, would never sell the inn. The inn was like another member of the family to him. It was their heritage and had been for more than a hundred and twenty years.

It would be like asking him to sell one of his daughters.

"The inn is not for sale," Andy informed the lawyer crisply.

"I'm afraid it has to be," Logan contradicted her in a calm voice that was making Andy crazy. "I just don't want to make this unpleasant."

"Too late," she told him coldly.

Dear Reader,

Looks like we've come to the end of our stay at Ladera by the Sea. I, for one, will miss wandering its sandy beach and sitting on the veranda, listening to the night sounds and the occasional whispers of young lovers.

This book belongs to Richard Roman's fourth and youngest daughter, Andrea. One semester away from graduating, Andy still doesn't know what career path she is going to take. Interested in everything—medicine, business, writing—she can't make up her mind. The only constant in her life, other than her family, is the inn. But one day a lawyer named Logan MacArthur arrives threatening to take it away. The state of California, in the interest of bringing in more revenue, declares eminent domain over the land the inn is standing on and just like that, the Roman way of life is threatened with extinction.

Well, not if Andy can help it. She and her sisters—the very pregnant Alex and Cris and the bride-to-be Stevi—begin a letter-writing campaign inundating Logan's senior law firm partners with stacks of letters of protest written by the friends and former guests of the inn. Logan comes by in person to make her cease and desist, but winds up being stuck at the inn himself, thanks to a flash flood making routes out of Ladera impassable. Logan begins to see firsthand what the inn means to the Romans and what *they* mean to the inn. He also learns that the impossibly infuriating Andy is not quite so impossible after all.

As always, I would like to thank you for taking the time to read my book, and from the bottom of my heart, I wish you someone to love who loves you back.

All good wishes,

Marie Ferrarella

HEARTWARMING

Saving Home

—

USA TODAY bestselling author

Marie Ferrarella

HARLEQUIN® HEARTWARMING™

Recycling programs
for this product may
not exist in your area.

ISBN-13: 978-0-373-36707-8

Saving Home

Printed in U.S.A.

Marie Ferrarella is a *USA TODAY* bestselling and RITA® Award-winning author who has written more than two hundred books for Harlequin, some under the name Marie Nicole. Her romances are beloved by fans worldwide. Visit her website, marieferrarella.com.

Books by Marie Ferrarella

HARLEQUIN HEARTWARMING

Ladera by the Sea

Innkeeper's Daughter
A Wedding for Christmas
Safe Harbor

Visit the Author Profile page
at Harlequin.com for more titles

To
Victoria
For
Her
Patience

PROLOGUE

THE PATH FROM the back of Ladera by the Sea, the family-owned, one-hundred-and-twenty-one-year-old bed-and-breakfast inn, to the small, private family cemetery far below was a little harder for Richard Roman to negotiate lately. The fault wasn't due to any subtle change in the inclined terrain, but to the less-than-subtle change in the way he'd been feeling of late.

It was as if someone had siphoned out all his available energy.

Still, he felt the need to make this pilgrimage down the hill so he could share his thoughts and feelings with the two people who had been so very close to him in life. The two people who still meant the world to him, even though both were now gone.

Richard was perfectly aware that he could do his "sharing" anywhere. All it took was the privacy of his own mind. But for him, it felt far more personal, as if he were still in touch with his Amy and with Dan, if he came here, to stand—or sit—between their two headstones and talk to them.

Reaching the bottom of the hill, Richard paused for a moment to catch his breath, something that had become trickier than it had been even a little while ago.

There was a seat carved into the base of the pine tree that stood like a sentry guarding the two graves. The seat had been created by his second daughter Cris's husband, Shane, so that he could stay here longer, if he so chose. Richard eased himself into it now.

He still hadn't caught his breath. Air seemed a little harder to draw in and out these days and he felt himself growing winded far faster than he was happy about. So far, he'd been able to keep this annoying change in his health from his four daughters, but he'd noticed that both Alex and Andy, his oldest and his youngest, had taken to looking at him thoughtfully.

Had they actually put the question to him, Richard would blame it on the fact that they were once more heading into their second busiest season of the year. Summers were first, but the approach of Christmas always ushered in a host of repeat guests who enjoyed celebrating at the inn.

And if that wasn't enough to explain why he appeared to be more harried than usual, he was also anticipating the pending births of not just one grandchild, but two. Alex and Cris were due within days of each other. That made this simultaneously a time for joy and a time of immense tension.

It was enough to give a man an occasional irregular heartbeat—or two.

The cherry on the sundae was Stevi's pending wedding. Mike, the former undercover DEA agent who had literally washed up on their shore at Stevi's feet, had recently decided to settle down here because "here" was where Stevi was. Now a homicide detective for the local police department, he'd proposed to her right in front of the entire family a moment before Thanksgiving dinner was served.

Stevi had been the wedding planner for her older sisters' double wedding but when it came to her own, surprisingly, she wanted something small and intimate.

"Knowing Stevi," Richard said, addressing the two tombstones that perforce took the place of Amy and Dan, "she'll probably wake up one morning, knock on all our doors and say something like, *If you want to come see me get married, you'd better get a move on because it's happening in half an hour.*"

He laughed softly to himself. "That's our Stevi," he said fondly to Amy. "Unconventional and spontaneous." He laughed again, but the laugh became a cough that took him several minutes to get under control.

"Sorry," he murmured, doing his best to regulate his breathing again. "I want to see Stevi married," Richard confided. "But between you and me, I'm hoping she holds off until after Alex and Cris have their babies. Maybe even after the first of the year," he added with a half smile. "Things calm down in January. It would be a perfect time for the wedding."

He rolled his eyes. "As if I could ever influence anything Stevi did. She's even more headstrong than Alex.

"Speaking of Alex," he continued, turning toward the headstone of his best friend, "it won't be long now before you're a grandpa, Dan. Who would have ever thought, during all those summers that you and your boy spent here, that someday Wyatt and Alex would be married, waiting for the birth of their first child? I certainly didn't, not with the way they were always trying to outdo each other, playing tricks when they weren't arguing." He shook his head. "Funny how things turn out, isn't it?"

The pain he'd been feeling off and on took a backseat to the ache he was experiencing right now. He would have given anything to spend even five more minutes in the actual company of his wife and best friend.

Richard's mouth curved as he allowed himself to remember another time, a time when his life had been so full of promise, of hope. Now it felt as if—for him—everything was in the process of winding down.

"I know you're probably sick of hearing this, but I miss you both so very much." He looked from one tombstone to the other. "The girls are wonderful, the men they've married or, in Stevi's case, are going to marry, are fine, upstanding young people, and my days and nights are filled with so many things to be grateful for. But I still miss you, still wish you were here to share in all this. Although, Dan, you trained me to only expect to see you a couple of times a year, with all those globe-trotting absences of yours, tracking down the next big story. Any more visits than that were a bonus."

Sadness seeped into Richard's smile. "Now there're no more bonuses, no more expectations."

Pausing, Richard blew out a breath. "Sorry, I didn't have any intentions of sounding so negative when I started to come down here for our visit—and yes, before you say anything, I know that the visits haven't been as regular but I seem to be lacking energy these days. Like the old joke goes, my get-up-and-go seems to have got-up-and-went. Guess I'm just getting old." He sighed.

"Okay, *older*," he amended, knowing that Dan would have taken him to task for that if he were here in more than just spirit. The late reporter maintained that "old" was always fifteen years older than the age you currently were.

Richard's eyes shifted to the headstone of his beloved Amy. He knew exactly what she would say right about now. "Yes, dear, I'll go see the doctor soon, but he'll say the same thing. That it's just old age. But to make you happy, I'll give him a call. Soon," he added with a wink.

Then, rising slowly to his feet, Richard glanced over to the path leading back up the incline to the inn and he squared his shoulders.

"See you two soon," he murmured, glancing over his shoulder at the graves.

A sharp twinge cut through him. It was gone the next second.

Getting old was a bear, Richard silently lamented as he started back to the inn.

The sky had been looking ominous all day. He wanted to make it back before it decided to rain.

CHAPTER ONE

SHE HAD A PROBLEM.

As far back as Andrea Roman could re-member, the month of December had been, by far, her very favorite time of year. The fourth daughter in a family of four girls, Andy had always been the effervescent one during the rest of the year, as well. She was always the one who not only saw the glass as being half full but who assumed it was about to be completely filled to the brim very soon.

Negativity and pessimism were just not part of her makeup.

That was why this strange, empty feel-ing gnawing away at her worried Andy as much as it did. She hadn't even felt this kind of prolonged, almost debilitating mal-aise after her mother died.

Back then, she'd devoted herself to

keeping her father's flagging spirits up. Granted, Andy had been very young at the time, but her sense of family, of loyalty, had always been exceptional.

Family still meant everything to her.

But these days, her family—her three older sisters—had moved on in different directions and she felt as if she was being left behind. She highly doubted any of her three sisters, Alexandra, Cristina or the soon to be married Stephanie, realized how she felt.

At least she hoped they didn't, Andy thought listlessly as she slowly walked around the inn.

Her insides ached and felt so hauntingly empty.

Empty despite the fact that the level of her activity had gone up several notches recently, the way it always did at this time of year. Empty despite the fact that both Alex and Cris were due to give birth very, very soon.

Or maybe the feeling of desolation was there *because* of all that.

Both of her oldest sisters were married,

and although Alex and Cris—and Wyatt and Shane, their respective husbands—all lived at the inn, each couple was involved in the creation of their own little family unit. Satellite units of the family they'd been born to.

The only family she knew, Andy thought as she slowly moved across the grass that Silvio, their gardener, kept so lush.

Andy supposed that she wouldn't have felt so desolate if Stevi was still unattached. Back before Mike had come into Stevi's life, it had been two against two, so to speak. She and Stevi on the one side while Alex and Cris were on the other.

But now Stevi was on the other side of the fence with Mike, her pending husband. And she was left to feel like a kid with her nose pressed up against the candy store window, allowed to see, but not to join in.

Oh, for her part she was crazy about all three of the men in her sisters' lives. She'd grown up with Alex's husband, Wyatt. They all had. During all those wild, wonderful summers when they were kids,

Wyatt had been like the big brother they never had.

But like them or not, having Wyatt, Shane and Mike here underscored that she was very much alone.

Of course, she'd dated a few guys herself, especially during the three and a half years she'd just spent in college—eclectically sampling several different majors and trying to find herself—but there had just never been anyone with that special something that told her this was the one. This was the guy she wanted to face forever with. A weekend, or a month, or even the summer, maybe. But forever? No, no way.

Maybe she'd been too picky. Andy turned around again, this time heading toward the back entrance. She'd promised Alex she'd take over the front desk and it was almost time to spell her very pregnant sister.

The dark rain clouds seemed to grow even darker with each step she took. It didn't help her mood.

If she lowered her standards, Andy

thought, still trying to wrestle this feeling of hopelessness to the ground, she'd be settling. And she didn't want to settle. At least not when it came to choosing a partner for life.

Andy frowned.

She absolutely hated feeling like this.

"What's up, Andy?" Alex asked, as she watched her making her way toward the reception desk. "You look like you've just lost your best friend."

"I have," Andy replied before she could censor herself. When was she going to learn to think things through before she spoke?

"Oh, I'm sorry," Alex told her, instantly sympathetic.

If nothing else, Andy thought, marriage and this pending pregnancy had turned her sometimes waspish, dictatorial, type-A sister into a kinder, more thoughtful version of herself.

"Who was it?" Alex coaxed. "Did I know her?"

"Me," Andy replied, looking away. She didn't want to make eye contact.

"Excuse me?"

"Me," Andy repeated. Resigned, she glanced up at Alex who was a shade taller than she was. "I just don't feel like myself anymore. It's like someone conducted a scorched earth policy inside me."

The old Alex instantly returned with a vengeance. Andy watched as her tall, temporarily un-slender sister snorted and shook her head.

"You want to talk about not feeling like yourself?" Alex challenged. "I feel like the Spanish Armada every time I try to negotiate going from here to there—never mind just standing up." She waved her hand. Since there were no guests in the reception area, Alex continued, working up a head of steam. "And my ankles, do you know how long it's been since I've seen my ankles? I have to take Wyatt's word for it that they're swollen because *I* certainly can't see them. All I know is that walking *anywhere* these days is a challenge."

Alex's blue eyes narrowed as she shot her sister an accusation. "I look at you with your skinny little body and it's everything

I can do not to drag you down to the pier and toss you into the ocean."

Andy forced a smile to her lips. She was deeply regretting having said a word to her sister.

But again, that still didn't change anything about the way *she* felt, Andy thought in mounting despair.

She wasn't exactly sure what possessed her, but Andy needed to make Alex understand. What she was experiencing had nothing to do with any sort of envy, but it was daunting and bordering on debilitating.

"Okay, I'm very sorry that you're going through all this, Alex, and everything you just complained about is probably true—"

"Probably?"

The single word was like waving a red flag in front of a bull.

"Probably?" Alex repeated, a flash of anger just beneath the surface.

Andy ignored all the very visible warning signs from her sister and pushed on. "But at the end of your temporary misshapen time as the Goodyear blimp's stand-in," she told Alex, "you're going to have a really amazing, mind-blowing prize for all your trouble. You're going to be holding a baby in your arms."

She couldn't contain the hopeless sigh that escaped her lips.

"Me, I'm going to go on feeling inadequate and adrift."

"Adrift?" Alex repeated incredulously, mocking Andy's choice of words. "Well, point your nose back toward home port, Melancholy Girl, because you're supposed to be taking over this front desk so I can eat and put my feet up before they get way too heavy for me to lift."

As Alex slid off the extra-padded, wide stool she'd been perched on, she caught a glimpse of Cris heading for the kitchen.

Perfect timing, Alex thought.

Cris had been the inn's resident chef for several years now, but as her own pregnancy had progressed, she had slowly—and reluctantly—been relinquishing some of her duties to Jorge, her chief assistant. Not to mention they'd hired a couple of part-timers who were currently working alongside of her.

Still, Richard Roman's second born was determined to continue working in at least a supervisory capacity for each and every meal prepared. Breakfast and dinner were included in the overall price of a room at the inn, lunch was not. But Cris still insisted on opening the kitchen in case any of the inn's guests felt like dining in.

As far as Cris was concerned, the inn took the place of home for guests. In this she and their father were of like mind.

Catching Cris's eye, Alex beckoned her over. She watched with a touch of envy as Cris seemed to maneuver with what appeared to be far less effort than *she'd* had to expend to cover the same ground.

This baby had her completely out of shape, Alex thought, frustrated.

When would this ordeal finally end so that she could have her life—not to mention her body—back? At this point, she was starting to feel as if she'd always been pregnant and there was no other way to be—no matter how much she wished there was.

"Hey, Cris," Alex began before the latter reached her. "You've been through this before, right?"

Where was this going? Cris wondered.

Of course she'd been through this before. She'd given birth to a son six years ago. Ricky. Named him after his grandfather. It still hurt her that Ricky's father had died halfway around the world, fighting for freedom, before he had ever set eyes on his son.

What was Alex getting at?

"I believe you know my son, your nephew," she replied, waiting for Alex to continue.

"If you've already been through this once," Alex said, underscoring the point, "how could you have willingly let it happen again? It's like being possessed by some alien life form that makes you go to the bathroom every ten and a half minutes. Why would you want to go through all this a second time?"

Andy bent over and addressed the very large bump that was to be her future niece or nephew. "She doesn't really mean it,

Baby. Your mother's just a very grumpy lady at times."

Glaring at her, Alex shifted her stomach away from Andy.

"Because," Cris told her older sister, acting as if the question was a perfectly logical one rather than something Alex's haywire hormones had made her spit out, "there is nothing in the world to equal the feeling of holding a baby in your arms for the very first time."

Alex was clearly not sold. "If that's all it is, you could get a part-time job volunteering on the maternity ward at the local hospital," she retorted.

Cris remained undaunted. "Talk to me after you've given birth to little whose-its-what's-it and see if you feel the same way," she told her older sister.

"I will," Alex promised.

"Now, if you'll excuse me, I have special lunch orders to oversee," Cris told them.

As she turned to continue to the kitchen, Cris glanced at the Christmas tree that the entire family—not to mention a number of the inn's paying guests—had spent the better part of the weekend putting up and decorating. Her eyes narrowed as she weighed its appearance.

"That side seems a little barren," she finally assessed, pointing toward a section that faced the kitchen rather than the front desk. She looked over her shoulder toward the only one of the three of them who could safely negotiate a ladder at this point. "Andy, could you do the honors?"

Andy was always one eager jump ahead of everything and everyone. So when she replied with a less than enthusiastic, "Sure, why not?" the response—more to the point, the *tone* of her sister's voice—made Cris immediately halt in her tracks.

She gave her younger sister a lengthy scrutiny. "Is there something wrong, Andy?"

Before Andy had a chance to reply, Alex spoke up for her, summarizing what she viewed was the problem.

"Apparently our little sister is battling a case of the doldrums."

Cris, her mothering instincts hardwired into her from birth, retraced her steps to

Andy. She paused to press her lips against her younger sister's forehead.

"You don't feel unduly warm," she judged, stepping back.

"That's because I'm not running a fever," Andy retorted, pulling her head back.

Cris stareded at her for what seemed like an eternity before she said, "No, you're not. You're also not smiling—or behaving anything like Andy." She tried a little humor to alleviate the situation. "Okay, who are you and what have you done with our little sister?"

"She's feeling sorry for herself," Alex said matter-of-factly.

For one of the few times in her life, Andy felt her temper flare. She banked it down successfully. However, she wasn't about to let the accusation go unanswered. "No, I'm not," Andy firmly denied.

Cris put her arm around Andy's shoulders in a move that fairly shouted camaraderie and protectiveness.

"Don't worry, honey, we all feel a little sorry for ourselves once in a while. It comes with the territory." Cris smiled broadly, glancing over in Alex's direction. "After all, we're related to Alex, which is enough of a reason for *anyone* to feel sorry for themselves." She winked at Andy.

The wink was not lost on Alex.

"Great, two against one," she complained to the world at large. Her eyes swept over the other two. "I can still take you on, you know."

"No one's taking anyone on," Cris told her calmly. "Especially not around Christmas."

Alex did her best to hide the knowing grin that was threatening to come out. "You're just saying that because I'd win."

Cris merely smiled the knowing smile that had always driven Alex crazy.

"If you say so," Cris replied accommodatingly. Then she turned toward Andy. "You want to come help me in the kitchen?"

Alex suddenly came to life. It was one thing to banter, but business was business and she wasn't in the mood to allow that to just slide. "Hey, Andy's supposed to be taking over for me at the front desk, remember?" The last of her question was directed toward Andy.

"Wyatt got you that extra-wide stool. Use it," Cris told her, nodding toward where it was parked beneath the reception desk.

Threading her arm around Andy's shoulders again, Cris gently guided her in the direction of the kitchen.

"It is *not* extra-wide," Alex cried defensively, raising her voice slightly. "It's just extra-comfortable, that's all."

"Either way," Cris answered without turning around this time, "use it. I need Andy. C'mon, I've got a chicken potpie in the refrigerator with your name on it." She knew it was Andy's favorite comfort food. "I'll heat it up and you can tell me what's bothering you."

Andy sighed as she walked into the kitchen beside her sister. "I don't really know what's bothering me."

That was, more or less, a lie. But she was not about to tell Cris that she was envious of her and the others, that she felt left out because she was a single to their doubles.

"Then we'll figure it out together,"

Cris proposed cheerfully. "Can't have my baby's godmother moping around like this, you know."

Andy frowned, confused. "I'm not Ricky's godmother."

There was a mischievous glimmer in Cris's eyes as she smiled and said, "No, you're not."

CHAPTER TWO

ANDY HESITATED JUST inside the kitchen door and suddenly reached for the counter to steady herself. Her breath caught in her throat as her brain kicked in, making the question she was about to ask Cris entirely unnecessary.

"Are you saying—?" Andy blew out a breath and tried again, this time hoping to be able to form a coherent, complete sentence. "You want me to be the new baby's godmother?"

"Only if you promise to learn how to speak English and not garbled gibberish," Cris qualified, doing her best to maintain a straight face.

"Absolutely!" Andy grabbed Cris's hands, as if that would somehow help her discern if her sister was just having fun with her or on the level. "Is Shane okay with this? I mean, did you ask him? Maybe he'd rather have someone else, or—"

Cris pulled her hands free from Andy's and placed her fingers against Andy's lips in an effort to, at least for the moment, stop the torrent of words.

"Shane is fine with this," Cris assured her. "In case you hadn't noticed, he's really crazy about this family." Resting her hand on the baby, who must have been once more attempting to kick its way out of her belly—a rather regular occurrence recently—the smile on Cris's lips widened. "I am an exceedingly lucky woman. To have two good men love me in one lifetime, well, it just doesn't get any better than that."

Andy saw that there were tears shimmering in Cris's eyes. Happy tears.

"No, it doesn't," Andy agreed quietly.

The next moment, Andy felt a wave of guilt wash over her. Guilt because she caught herself being envious of Cris.

Her tall, willowy, gentle older sister had had two men pledge to love her forever. Two men who vowed to be there for her so she would have someone to lean on. Not that she didn't think Cris deserved the love of both her late husband and Shane, the man she'd married last Christmas. She did.

But was it too much to ask to have someone like that come *her* way?

Apparently, Andy decided, it was. She struggled to suppress a deep sigh.

Cris pressed her lips together, knitting her eyebrows into one very thoughtful line. "For a second there, you seemed like the old Andy," she told her sister. "But then this new Andy 2.0 version popped out again." Cris gave her a penetrating stare—and a warning. "You might as well resign yourself to the fact that you're not coming out of this kitchen until you get it all off your chest."

Andy just looked at her.

Cris shook her head. "And sorry, I'm not a sucker for that sad, little girl lost face you just put on. Now talk to me, kid. Let it all out. You'll feel better."

Andy shrugged, watching Jorge, Cris's sous-chef, move about the kitchen on what seemed like automatic pilot. Cris was the creative one in the kitchen. These days, as she was getting closer to her due date, Jorge had gone so far as to insist that he wouldn't listen to a thing she said unless she was sitting down when she said it.

As independent as her sisters, but less vocal about it, Cris had no choice but to comply.

Apparently Jorge's stubbornness was on the same level as Alex's. Cris had lamented that she was outnumbered, but Andy believed her sister was secretly grateful for all the help she was getting. It was to the point where everyone was anticipating—correctly—her next order.

Andy blew out a breath, surrendering. "All right, if you really want to know…"

"I do," Cris replied firmly.

It took Andy a second to gather her courage. She wasn't one given to whining or complaining. "For the first time in my life, I feel like I'm the odd girl out."

"Well, there's no arguing that you're a little odd," Cris allowed, then she laughed, her eyes crinkling with unabashed humor. "In comparison to the rest of us, you've always been the one on an even keel, the one who was always happy. You're the one who always makes the world seem a little brighter, a little happier because of your attitude."

Cris grew more serious as she made her way to the industrial-sized refrigerator that her father had had installed two renovations ago, at the time it became clear that the one they had could no longer accommodate all the food they needed to feed their increased number of guests.

"Go on. Don't stop," Cris urged. "There's got to be more to it than that." She took out one of the potpies she'd made earlier that morning and popped it into the microwave. Hitting the appropriate numbers, Cris turned around to look at her sister. "You were saying—?" she coaxed.

Andy wet her very dry lips before continuing. "You and Alex and Stevi, you've got your men. You're set for life, for having your own families."

This wasn't coming out right. It was making her seem petty and small, and she wasn't, she thought, annoyed with herself.

She would have gladly laid her life down for any of her sisters or her father. That list also included her brothers-in-law as well as her nephew.

She was feeling this way because she wanted to *be just like them*, to have the promise of love and a family—her *own* family.

"And me," she continued out loud, "I'm going to be your kids' crazy old Aunt Andy."

"Wait," Cris said. "Shouldn't there be violins for this part? And a blizzard? Definitely need a blizzard to sell this."

Andy flushed. "You're making fun of me," she complained dejectedly.

"Damn straight I am," Cris answered, crossing back to her for a moment. "Andy, love doesn't punch a clock or have some kind of a mysterious, preset timetable. Some people find the person they were meant to be with early on, others don't until years later—"

"And some never do," Andy pointed out. And she was certain that she belonged to that group.

"Granted, some never do. But that's not going to be you, kid," Cris said with complete conviction.

"There's no guarantee on that," Andy protested.

"Yes, there is. *I* guarantee that there'll be someone for you soon enough," Cris told her fiercely.

But Andy shook her head. She wasn't a kid anymore. She didn't believe in fairy tales.

"Don't argue with a pregnant woman, Andy. Don't you know that aggravation might make me go into premature labor?"

"No, it can't." Then Andy considered Cris nervously. "Can it?" she asked in a far less certain voice.

"She is pulling your legs," Jorge interjected, taking pity on the youngest Roman sister.

"Leave my legs alone, Cris," Andy said, picking up on Jorge's slight mangling of the saying.

"Okay, I will," Cris agreed. "But only if you cease and desist feeling sorry for yourself for no reason. Part of the fun in life, Andy, is the journey." She patted her cheek. "Enjoy the journey and don't be so impatient—"

"Said the woman who's been staring impatiently at her belly. Don't you know that a watched belly doesn't go into labor?" Stevi asked with a grin, crossing over to the long worktable. She'd come into the kitchen in time to hear the last exchange and quickly made her own judgment on the nature of the discussion.

Looking at Stevi, Cris shook her head. "There's so much wrong with that, I don't even know where to begin. There you go," she declared, momentarily changing the subject as she put a steaming, individual serving of chicken potpie in front of Andy, who was already seated on a stool at the long table. Turning back to Stevi, she asked, "And just what brings you here, invading my kitchen?"

"Other than the wonderful aroma of one of your chicken potpies?" Stevi asked, a deliberately innocent expression on her face.

"Other than that," Cris conceded. "By the way, if you want one—"

"I do," Stevi assured her with feeling.

"There just happens to be another one in the refrigerator. I'll heat it up for you." Moving slowly toward the fridge, Cris asked, "You were saying, Stevi?"

Her mind on lunch, Stevi had temporarily lost her train of thought. "I was?"

Cris turned to fix Stevi with a look. "About what drew you over here," she prompted.

"Oh, right." Stevi nodded. "Now I remember. Alex sent me in here, told me to tell Andy to get her sorry little behind out to the reception area pronto like she was supposed to."

Andy began to rise, but Cris waved her back into her seat. "Tell our illustrious pregnant Napoleon that Andy will come out after she's had her lunch."

"Sure thing," Stevi agreed, then added with a grin, "After I have mine."

Cris exchanged glances with Stevi. They were all aware of what was going to happen next. "You do know that she's going to come waddling in here, throwing her weight around and issuing orders."

Stevi shrugged that off. For the most part, it was a given. Alex had a tendency to take on the role of team leader as well as unofficial mother ever since their mom had died. She frequently overstepped her boundaries, but her heart, the others reluctantly agreed, was in the right place.

"She's not as fierce now that she's eight and a half months pregnant," Stevi commented with a laugh.

"Oh yes, she is," Andy replied, rolling her eyes as she blew on her forkful of food.

Cris laughed and took out the second potpie. She gave it to Stevi, who happily dug in.

"Since when has the kitchen turned into a black hole?" Alex demanded as she stormed into the kitchen half a second after Stevi took her first bite.

Instinctively Cris put herself between Alex and their two younger sisters. "Black hole? What are you talking about?"

"Well, what would you call it?" Alex shot back. She gestured impatiently at Stevi and Andy. "People go in, but they don't come out."

"Offhand, I'd call it trying to get away from Alex's mini reign of terror," Cris answered, her eyes meeting Alex's. The latter raised her chin as if bracing for another go-round.

Andy smiled to herself. She'd missed this, missed the bantering, the pseudo-bravado where each of them tried to outdo the others. But underneath it all, they didn't really mean anything that was said.

Still, anyone listening in might be hard pressed to believe how quickly they could all be galvanized into a united front if one of them happened to be threatened from the outside.

Like the time Cris's former in-laws wanted to take legal custody of Ricky, their late son's child. The entire family, including Wyatt, had banded together to keep that from happening. They'd won, too.

Cris cast an eye toward Andy, aware that she'd fallen silent. Silent, but not sullen, Cris noted, pleased. Alex's flare-up was temporarily placed on the back burner.

"I see that you're smiling again," Cris noted triumphantly.

Alex looked over at Andy, then made a dismissive noise. "That's not a smile, that's a grimace," she said, correcting Cris. "She must have found a chicken bone in that pie you're always making."

"There are no bones in my chicken pot-pies," Cris replied calmly and authoritatively.

Alex gazed down at the pies her sisters were systematically consuming. "I guess I'd better eat one to make sure." She looked around. "If I can find a stool in here that's built to accommodate someone larger than a Smurf."

"Make that ten Smurfs," Stevi murmured, under her breath but deliberately loud enough to be overheard.

Alex glared at Stevi. "Are you saying I'm fat?"

"No, I'm saying that you're a little bigger than ten Smurfs. You are, you know," Stevi pointed out with a straight face. "Can't argue that."

"Whereas you would give arguing with the devil a shot," Andy said.

"Quiet, pipsqueak. Eat your pie," Stevi

ordered, gesturing to her plate. She turned her attention back to Alex, who was about to savor the first forkful of her own pie. "What about the reception desk?"

Alex raised one shoulder in a half shrug. "It's not unattended."

Cris glanced at the long worktable, although it wasn't really necessary. All four of them were present and accounted for. That brought up a very logical question. "So who's minding the reception desk?" The next second, the answer hit her. She glared at Alex. "You didn't drag out poor Dad and tell him to do it, did you?"

"Of course not," Alex said, taking offense. "Dorothy volunteered." The inn's head housekeeper had been with them for years. "Speaking of Dad," Alex went on, "does anyone else think he's looking rather pale lately?"

"Yes, but you know Dad. He always pushes himself too hard around this time of year," Cris reminded them.

"I think keeping busy helps him cope with not having Mom around at Christmas," Stevi's face lit up as memories began to crowd her head. "Remember how special she always made the holidays? Even the little things. When she did them, they became almost magical," she recalled fondly.

"I hope you're right about Dad," Alex murmured.

She worried about him a great deal. After their mother had died, there was a period of time when he'd fallen ill and they were all afraid that they would lose him, as well. He'd rallied, but the image of a frail man was never far from any of their minds.

"Still," Alex continued, "I think we should all gang up on him and make Dad get a physical—just in case."

"You know him," Andy pointed out. "He'll just tell us not to worry, that everything's fine and that'll be the end of it."

"That *used* to be the end of it," Alex said, then added with a touch of smugness, "but we've got muscle now."

"What are you talking about?" Stevi asked, staring at Alex as if she had just gone off the deep end.

Alex gave her a look that all but said *keep up.*

"We could actually physically *carry* Dad to the doctor's office." Alex could tell she'd lost her sisters. "Don't you see? We've got Wyatt, Shane and Mike. That's three against one. *They* could certainly get Dad over to Dr. Donnelly's office for a thorough check up."

"You're talking about kidnapping the man," Cris said, shaking her head. "That's a last resort," she said, "using the guys to get Dad to the doctor's office. You have to leave the man some dignity."

"Dignity's the last thing a person thinks about if they land in a hospital bed," Alex insisted. "And I'm trying to prevent that."

Stevi shook her head. "God, I hope the baby doesn't get your optimism."

Alex drew herself up a little taller. "I'm being realistic."

"What you're being," Stevi countered, "is a dark cloud."

Andy shook her head at that and laughed. "So what else is new?"

Instead of a defensive remark, or a put down from Alex the way she expected, Andy saw her oldest sister grow perfectly still, almost like a deer caught in the head-lights.

"Alex?" Andy leaned in closer as she studied her sister's tense face and rigid body. Alex was *never* this still for this long. "Talk to me. Is something wrong?"

"Is it the baby?" Stevi asked with a note of panic.

Jorge had abandoned the giant salad he was preparing to hurry over to the work-table. A father himself three times over, he watched Alex solicitously, ready to be of assistance.

"Say something," Cris pleaded, taking her hand.

Alex squeezed back—hard—but only made a strange, unidentifiable noise. After another several seconds had passed, she let out a long, shaky breath. Her free hand was still possessively covering her belly.

She waited, but the pain didn't return. Her relief was unimaginable.

"False alarm," she told her sisters and Jorge, offering them a rather weak, tired smile to accompany the words. And then she added in a smaller, equally hopeful voice, "I think."

CHAPTER THREE

THERE WAS A thin line of perspiration running along Alex's hairline. "Maybe you should see your doctor," Andy suggested, as they all remained huddled around the worktable in the kitchen, partially finished potpies forgotten in the scare of Alex's possible labor pains.

Back to her old self, Alex shook her head. "I'm not due until the end of the month, and right now I don't have the time," she said, brushing the incident off.

"*Make* the time," Cris told her pointedly.

"What I'm going to make is tracks before you *all* gang up on me," Alex replied. Using the worktable for support, she began to push herself up to her feet.

"You're as bad as Dad," Cris continued. "How can you even think of forcing him to go to the doctor when you won't consider going yourself?"

Stevi placed her hand gently but firmly on Alex's shoulder. "Sit," she ordered. "Finish eating."

"I have to get back to the reception desk," Alex argued.

"No, you don't," Andy said. She had finished both her impromptu lunch and feeling sorry for herself. It was time to make herself useful. "I'll go." She stood. "Take as long as you like. Great potpie, Cris— as always."

Cris merely smiled as she reached for the empty pie plate.

Jorge managed to insert himself between the pie plate and the woman he considered his boss. He deposited it in the sink and proceeded to wash it.

"You are working too hard, Miss Cris," he told her simply.

Cris knew better than to argue with Jorge. Given the opportunity, he could go on and on for hours until he won his point. It was far easier just to go along with him.

"Thank you, Jorge."

It was the last thing Andy heard as she left the kitchen.

SHE HURRIED THROUGH the dining area, noting that several of the inn's guests had trickled into the room. Jasmine, the college student who was their part-time waitress, was busy taking their orders.

It looked as if Cris was going to be busy for a little while, Andy mused. It was a good thing her sister had Jorge as her assistant. He was quick and competent and, most important, he wouldn't allow Cris to work too hard no matter what she said.

The only person currently in the reception area when Andy got there was Dorothy.

Like most of the small staff at the inn, Dorothy had a story. The woman had checked into the inn for an overnight stay—the last one, she had believed, that she would spend on this earth. It had been luck that brought Richard Roman to her door to check on her before he turned in for the night.

And instinct that had kept him there, talking with the lonely, distraught woman until well past dawn.

That dawn had signaled a new beginning for Dorothy. Richard Roman had a knack for sensing who needed support and who needed nothing more than a meal and a pat on the back. He offered Dorothy a place to stay for as long as she needed it. More than that, he had offered the woman hope.

Twenty-five years later, Dorothy was still living and working at the inn. Along the way, she had become part of the family in every sense of the word.

Seeing Andy, the woman looked at her with concern. "Is Alex all right? She was a little pale when she left here."

"Alex *is* pale. But I think she's just very impatient to have all this behind her," Andy confided.

Dorothy chuckled under her breath. "You're probably right." She tucked the well-worn paperback novel she'd been reading back into the oversized pocket of her apron. She didn't like being idle for long. "What can I do for you?"

"It's what *I* can do for *you*," Andy corrected her. "I'm here to take over the desk."

Had this been in the middle of the morning, she would have quickly relinquished the duty.

"If you have something else you need to do, I can stay here a little longer," Dorothy said. "I don't mind. All the beds are made, the rooms are cleaned."

They were almost booked up, which meant that most of the various rooms and suites were filled.

"I don't know how you do it, Dorothy." Andy shook her head. "Anyone else would still be making beds. If I *ever* move away, I'm taking you with me."

"Are you?" Dorothy asked before clarifying, "Moving away?"

"Maybe," Andy replied.

Wasn't that what people did after graduation? Moved away? Of course, none of her sisters had. They'd just become integrated into the business of running the inn. Alex handled bookings and the business end, Cris manned the kitchen and Stevi did the on-site event planning.

With her future in a state of flux, Andy shrugged helplessly. "I don't know. Everything's such a big question mark."

"You have one semester to go before you graduate." It wasn't a question. Dorothy kept close tabs on everything that went on in the lives of the family she'd adopted. The family that had taken her in when she most needed to attach herself to something solid. She was certain that Richard, and subsequently his daughters, had saved her life. As far as she was concerned, her life was theirs.

"I know," Andy replied. Even to her own ears, her tone didn't reflect an eagerness to get her degree and get on with her life. Her voice sounded rather hollow and empty.

"It's only natural to be confused, dear, frightened of what lies ahead of you in the next few months and years." Dorothy gave her a heartening smile. "Feeling that way, Andy, doesn't mean that you're going crazy."

Andy's eyes widened. "How did you know?" she asked incredulously.

"Because almost everyone goes through

that—if they're lucky. The future can be a scary place."

"Lucky?" How could feeling this nameless confusion be considered lucky?

"Yes. The ones who aren't lucky, who don't feel scared, are the ones whose future has been dictated and sewn up for them right from the moment they first drew breath. They're the ones whose choices are limited and whose options are nonexistent."

Andy considered what she'd said. "Put that way, I guess I am lucky."

"Absolutely," Dorothy confirmed with a good measure of enthusiasm. "The whole world is opening up for you, Andy. You can be anything you want to be."

"Anything, huh?" Andy asked, a touch of mischief shimmering in her eyes. "What if I want to be a six-foot-tall, skinny brunette model?"

"You can be *almost* anything you want to be," Dorothy amended without skipping a beat. Twenty-five years in the family had taught the woman to be ready for anything.

Andy laughed, brushing her lips against

the housekeeper's soft cheek. "I love you, Dorothy."

The housekeeper looked immensely pleased. She'd heard this declaration from the girls more than once. However, each time was special, as touching for her as the very first time she had ever heard the words.

Andy, barely a toddler, had been the first to say *I love you*. They were grown women now, but they were *her* grown women even if she didn't share a surname or their blood.

"I love you right back," Dorothy told her, slipping off Wyatt's stool. "Remember, call me if you need anything."

"Don't I always?" Andy asked innocently.

Dorothy snorted in response. "You're just as stubborn as your sisters so, no, I'm sure you don't."

"I'll work on that," Andy promised, and then a thought hit her. "Okay, here's something you can do for me—and I'd really appreciate it if you did."

"I'm listening."

"I want you to quietly look in on Dad," Andy told her.

"Because?" Dorothy asked.

Andy shrugged, knowing that the request sounded a little strange—maybe she was worrying for nothing. But having Dorothy confirm that would go a long way toward making her feel better. "Just to see if he's okay."

Dorothy cocked her head, scrutinizing her. "Why wouldn't he be?"

Andy shrugged again. "Something is off about Dad. He's slowed down lately, like there's some big rock pressing down on him, taking the zip out of his step."

Dorothy smiled indulgently. "It's called getting older, dear."

"Maybe," Andy said. But she really didn't believe it. Granted, her father could never have been accused of being an athletic go-getter. He certainly wasn't anywhere near as full of life as Alex and Stevi. Still, her father had always been slow but steady, like the tortoise in the fable.

"But I'd feel better if you peeked in on him," Andy said. She gave Dorothy a plaintive look, one that had never failed to melt the housekeeper's kind heart.

As if Dorothy could ever say no to any of them. She nodded. "Consider him peeked in on," she said as she left reception and went in search of Andy's father.

There were no new guests checking in and, according to the roster, there wouldn't be any arriving until around noon the next day.

It took Andy all of about thirty seconds to remember Cris's comment about the Christmas tree needing more decorations on the one side.

That was easy enough to do, she thought. And while she enjoyed the camaraderie of decorating the tree with everyone else in the family, there were times when she savored doing things alone.

This felt as if she was carving out a niche for herself. Okay, it was only a niche partially filled with decorations and a couple of barren branches belonging to a Scotch pine. But it was her niche.

Andy dragged the ladder out of the hall closet where it had been stashed after they'd brought the tree in on the first of December and finished the decorating. Well, almost finished it.

Once she had the ladder next to the tree, she snapped it into place and made certain that all the tabs that needed to be locked *were* locked.

Arming herself with decorations, Andy carefully made her way up the aluminum ladder as far as she could. She stopped one step short of the very top.

With a critical, artistic eye, she went about hanging the decorations where she thought they would be the most effective.

As she worked, Andy silently upbraided herself for her earlier descent into a funk. She was well aware that life wasn't all roses, gumdrops and music. But as far as things went, she knew she was one of the lucky ones and to regard her life as anything but privileged was just plain wrong.

Stretching up on the tips of her toes to reach a bare spot, Andy thought she heard the front door open.

Unable to see the entrance Andy listened intently, waiting to hear someone call out.

No one did.

When she didn't discern anything further, Andy decided it had just been her imagination. She got back to critically analyzing where to place decorations.

"Excuse me?"

Andy was so wrapped up in what she was doing, the deep male voice coming from both behind her and beneath her made her jump.

It wasn't advisable, she realized the next moment, for anyone perched on the next-to-the-top step of a ladder to jump.

The ladder started to wobble and tip. Andy saw too late that there was nothing to brace herself against. She couldn't very well grab on to the Christmas tree to steady herself, not without bringing the tree down on top of her.

Faster than it took her to gasp, Andy found herself airborne, separating from the ladder, which was falling with her.

She braced herself for a hard impact, but while she was shaken and the air was knocked out of her, she did not come crashing down onto the floor.

Instead, she found herself in the very strong, outstretched arms of the man with the deep voice.

The man who was to blame for this embarrassing incident in the first place.

As she landed in his arms, she felt his forearms tensing, becoming so hard they could have been made of steel.

It took her a second to get her brain in gear. When she did, Andy found herself studying the face of an exceedingly handsome man of about thirty-two with intense sky-blue eyes, trim, dark blond hair and near-perfect chiseled features.

She had never seen him before in her life. His was not a face she would have forgotten.

"Are you all right?" he asked.

Andy hated being caught off guard, hated being perceived as vulnerable in any way. It went against her own image of herself. This damsel-in-distress scenario was far from her liking.

"I would have been more all right," she informed the man, "if you hadn't snuck up on me."

"Sorry. I left my noisy shoes at home," he said matter-of-factly. "There didn't seem to be anyone around."

"Obviously your assessment of the situation turned out to be wrong."

"Obviously," he agreed.

Andy twisted her head and looked to see if the ladder had done any damage when it landed. Mercifully, it had managed to go straight down and was on the floor in front of the Christmas tree. None of the balls or decorations had been broken or dislodged.

That's when Andy realized the stranger was still holding her. "Would you mind putting me down?" she asked.

"Is that a request or a question?"

He wanted to debate this? Andy felt her back go up. "What's the difference?"

"If it's a request, I have to comply. If it's a question, all I have to do is give you an answer."

Andy stared at him. Bemused and puzzled, she said, "And if it's the latter?"

"Then I'd say yes, I do mind."

Okay, she'd had about enough of this

wise guy. Granted, he'd broken her fall, but he was the one responsible for it in the first place, so the two canceled each other out.

She narrowed her eyes. "Put me down."

He inclined his head. "Yes, ma'am."

Lowering her until her feet touched the floor, the stranger released his hold. Rather than say anything, he turned his attention to the ladder. He righted it with ease. "Looks like there's no harm done to either you or the ladder," he told her. Before she could contest his evaluation, he asked, "Could you tell me where I might find Mr. Richard Roman?"

Andy raised her chin. The guy couldn't miss her combative stance, she hoped. "I could."

After several moments had gone by without any further information from her, he asked, "*Would* you tell me where I can find Mr. Roman?"

"That all depends," she told him.

His eyes narrowed uncertainly. "On what?"

"On the reason that you're looking for him," Andy answered.

"I'm afraid that's between Mr. Roman and, for now, me."

CHAPTER FOUR

UNDER ORDINARY CIRCUMSTANCES, Andy would have just called someone—Dorothy most likely—to take this man to her father's office, or in a pinch, taken him there herself.

But there was something about him, something that made her uneasy. And it wasn't because he was probably the best-looking man she'd ever seen. Her brothers-in-law, Wyatt and Shane, and her future brother-in-law, Mike, were all very striking men, but this stranger had an almost classic air about him. A layer of polish that was impossible to miss.

At the same time, the stranger made her feel as if she needed to protect her father from him, despite the fact that she hadn't a clue as to why the man wanted to see her father.

For all she knew, her dad might have won the lottery and this man was here to present him with a lump-sum check.

But she strongly doubted it.

Prepared to stare him down, barring his path and access to the rest of the inn until she had her answers, Andy heard a noise behind her.

A whiff of Alex's perfume preceded her sister a moment before Andy heard Alex ask, "Is there a problem here?"

"I certainly hope not," the tall blond stranger said politely, and then he smiled at Alex. "Maybe you can help me. I'm looking for Richard Roman."

"I believe he's in his office at the moment," Alex said, sliding onto the stool behind the reception desk. "Andy, why don't you bring this gentleman to Dad's office?"

Andy didn't move a muscle. "Is he expecting you?"

"I really don't think so," he replied, unfazed by the challenge in her voice and body language.

Just as she'd thought. The man was probably a pushy real estate agent. It wouldn't be the first time a developer had attempted to buy the inn out from under them. She and her sisters all loved the inn, but to her father, it was a living, breathing entity, a piece of his heritage. The inn was part of him.

The suit this stranger had on was expensive. Obviously he was good at what he did.

Andy didn't trust him a whit.

"Then why don't you give me your name and number and I'll have my father call you at his convenience," she suggested.

"Andy, that's not how Dad does business," Alex chided. "I'm sorry. She's still rather new at all this."

"I understand," he replied, offering a smile that went a long way to lighting up the immediate area.

"I'm glad you do, but I'm afraid I don't—*we* don't," Andy said stubbornly, slanting an annoyed glance in Alex's direction. "Now, if you're not going to tell us why you want to see my father, I'm afraid we're going to have to go back to plan B."

"Which is?" the stranger asked gamely.

"You giving us your name and my father calling you when he has the time," she repeated.

Andy didn't care for the look that came over the man's features. As if he knew something she didn't. "Trust me, he'll want to make time for this," he assured her.

That was when she noticed that he was carrying a briefcase. A briefcase that he now patted.

The pieces came together in her head. "You're a lawyer, aren't you?"

His smile was incredibly sensual. Andy didn't know which annoyed her more, his amusement or his sensuality.

"What makes you say that?" he asked.

He didn't bother denying that he was a lawyer. "Because only a lawyer could get under my skin this fast."

Her eyes narrowed as she considered the stranger from an entirely different perspective. Now he wasn't just an annoying person who wouldn't give her his name, he represented a possible problem, the nature of which was still unclear.

"What's this all about?"

"Currently, it's about you not letting me see your father," he replied calmly.

"He's a very busy man," Andy informed the guy coldly. She was aware that Alex was staring at her, but she ignored her sister. "We can't just let anyone waltz in and interrupt what he's doing. Now either state your business or give me your card and I'll have him—"

"Give me a call at his convenience, yes, you've already covered that," the lawyer said, clearly tiring of this game.

Well, he was the one who started the cat-and-mouse by not giving them his name. It was the oddest way to request a business meeting she'd ever heard of.

"I assure you that your father is definitely going to want to talk to me, Miss Roman. My name is MacArthur. Logan MacArthur."

Andy glared at all six foot two of the man.

The lawyer cast an impeccable silhouette, and if she knew anything about clothes—and she did—the suit the man had on was roughly equal in price to her entire wardrobe.

He seemed to be someone born to privilege. Andy had an instinctive reaction to people who behaved that way.

She didn't like them.

He looked her right in the eye. "*Now* may I see your father?"

"No," Andy answered.

Her answer surprised her sister. The expression on Logan MacArthur's face was impossible to read.

"*Now* you can tell me what this is all about and why you want to talk to him."

"Is she always this protective?" Logan asked, turning to Alex.

"I don't know," Alex confessed with a vague shrug. "Most of the time she's in school."

Andy's eyes blazed. She didn't care for the way Alex's reply reduced her to the state of an adolescent whose actions had no logic.

"Are you always this secretive?" she challenged MacArthur. Something was off, she could feel it. *Why* was he being so cagy?

Alex had had enough. "Andy, watch the

desk. I'll take Mr. MacArthur to Dad's office."

Andy frowned. Every step was an effort for Alex these past few weeks and seeing her ponderously make her way to the back of the inn would be an oppressive weight on her conscience.

Andy blew out a beleaguered breath. "You stay where you are, Alex," she said curtly. "I'll take him."

Alex shifted off the stool and motioned Andy over.

"You're sure?" Alex asked in a lowered voice, regarding her uncertainly. "You're not going to lead him through the back entrance down to the beach, are you?"

"Don't tempt me." There wasn't even a glimmer of a smile on her lips. Stepping away, she crossed directly in front of Logan and said, "Let's go."

"Yes, ma'am," he replied, falling in behind her. "Nice tree," he commented as they passed the Christmas tree.

"Thank you!" Alex called.

Since she was the one he'd found on the ladder, putting the finishing touches on the oversize Christmas tree, he'd meant the comment for the firebrand who was leading him.

"Did you do all the decorating?" he asked. "Or are you the kind who delegates?"

Andy spared him one uninterested glance before looking straight ahead again. "You don't have to make small talk."

"I was just curious."

"I guess a lot of questions aren't being answered today," she snapped.

He laughed in response, despite the fact that he could tell his amusement didn't sit well with Andy. But at the moment, there was nothing she could do about it.

The door to her father's office was closed. She knocked on it lightly. "Dad? Are you there?" When there was no reply, she knocked again, just as lightly as before. Still no answer.

The young woman turned and said, "Looks like you're out of luck after all, MacArthur. He's not in."

She turned on her heel. He remained in front of the door.

"Where else would he be?" Logan asked.

If looks could kill, present company would have been reduced to a pile of smoldering embers. "I'm sorry, he didn't file his itinerary with me this morning so I really haven't a clue. Seems like you're going to have to leave your card with me, after all."

Oh, no. I'm not making it that easy for you, Logan thought. "I have a feeling if I did that, it might just inspire you to test out your shredder."

"We don't have a shredder," she informed him. "But now that you mention it, that is something to think about." Again she moved away from the door—and again, Logan didn't follow.

"If you don't mind, I'll just sit in your father's office," he nodded at the door, "and wait for him there."

She did *not* want this man in her father's office, hovering about like some vulture waiting for its prey to die so it could start eating.

"No telling how long you'll have to wait," she warned him.

"I don't mind," Logan told her flatly. "I'm being well compensated for my time."

Andy struggled to keep her temper in check, something that ordinarily wasn't a problem for her.

But she absolutely hated not knowing why he was here. There was something about this man and his perfectly groomed exterior that made her nervous, as if something was going to happen, something that she wouldn't be able to fix.

People with nothing to hide were far more open than he was being. Granted, he'd said he was a lawyer and lawyers were closemouthed unless they were on the floor of a courtroom, grandstanding and thrilling to the sound of their own voices. At least that was how they were portrayed on TV, which was the closest she'd come to seeing a lawyer before this.

But this was about her father, and whatever affected Richard Roman affected them all. They were a family that didn't keep secrets from one another. That wasn't what they were all about.

Obviously this man didn't understand that simple concept.

She tried to approach the problem from a basic, practical perspective, hoping that would finally sink in. "Well, I can't just leave you alone in my father's office."

Logan nodded and for one brief, shining moment, Andy thought she was finally going to get rid of the man. But then he said, "You could stay with me, make sure I didn't make off with anything."

"What I'm worried about," she replied, doing her best to inject an eerie stillness in her voice that she hoped he recognized as the calm that came just before a huge storm, "is that you're going to say something to upset my father. My father has enough to deal with these days."

"Oh? Like what?" Logan asked, a bit too innocently in her opinion.

She gave him an answer steeped in practicality and logic. Something she felt would appeal to the man. "This is one of our busiest times of the year and my father prides himself on always making sure everyone who stays here has an exceptionally good time. That's not nearly as easy as it sounds."

"I'm sure it's not." He was nothing if not sympathetic sounding.

Andy saw his attitude as something else. "Do you get bonuses for patronizing people? Or is that just an extra you throw in?" she wanted to know.

The woman was clearly imagining things, but he wasn't going to call her out on it. He had an endless supply of patience and he dug deep into it right now.

"I wasn't aware I was being patronizing."

"Well, now you know," Andy informed him with finality.

"I do apologize," Logan told her, trying to suppress his amusement. He couldn't help himself. With her tough attitude, this very young woman should be working in the military. Or teaching self-defense somewhere, anyway.

As hard as he tried to choke back a smile, she must've sensed something in his expression. He watched her bristle. *Uh-oh.*

Andy found his smile unsettling, which

in itself annoyed her to no end. Given half a chance, she would have liked to wipe it off the man's chiseled face.

"If you're really serious about apologizing," she said, "just leave."

From the way he crossed his arms and leaned against the doorframe, she could tell that was not about to happen. "I'm afraid I can't," he responded. "Not without first seeing your father."

This was getting her nowhere. They were going around in circles and he looked as if he was enjoying the process.

"I could have our head of security make you go," she threatened him.

It was an empty threat because there *was* no head of security, although in a pinch, she felt she could turn to Silvio. Their long-time gardener was well versed in things that a gardener had no business knowing. But then, Silvio hadn't always been a gardener. The life he'd led before being forced to flee his native country was very different from his life here at the inn.

"He could try," Logan told her in a mild voice. The expression on his handsome face told her that a mere head of security—even if one existed—couldn't remove him from the premises.

Maybe it was because she felt so edgy, or maybe it was because she was struggling with those momentary twinges of envy, feeling the odd woman out. She really didn't know. But whatever was behind her reaction to this man and his mysterious need to communicate only with her father, Andy felt her normally large supply of patience swiftly evaporating.

"Why won't you tell us what business you have with my father?" she demanded.

"Because the business is with *your father*," he underscored firmly without so much as raising his voice. "After I've discussed it with him, if your father chooses to include you in the matter, that's his call to make and *his* business. My orders are to speak directly—and only—to him."

"My father doesn't keep secrets from his family," she informed him.

"You're very fortunate. Not all families are like that," he added with what Andy felt was a momentary break in the cool, calm facade she'd been dealing with. "However, it doesn't change a thing."

Andy stood there for a long moment, struggling hard to keep her temper in check as well as banking down the torrent of words that felt as if they were rushing to her tongue.

Taking a deep breath, she forced herself to study the man before her.

Just what was it that made him tick? What was his story? she couldn't help wondering.

There was no hard-and-fast reason for her to suspect that he would upset her father. She knew she was being overprotective because she worried about him. But, be that as it may, she still couldn't shake the gut feeling that the man she was dealing with represented trouble with a capital *T*.

Get a grip.

The sooner this was over, the better for everybody, she decided. Opening the door to the office, she gestured inside, surprising Logan if his expression was any indication.

As he crossed the threshold, Andy took

her cell phone out of her back pocket and tapped out her father's number on the keypad. It was by far the fastest way she knew to locate her father and get him to come to his office.

This time, however, it proved an unproductive way to locate him. The moment she heard the call go through and the sound of ringing begin on her end, she also heard the corresponding sound of a ringing phone—and it was coming from the top drawer of her father's desk.

Logan looked from the desk to her, raising a quizzical eyebrow. "I take it your father's not hiding under the desk for some reason."

Andy sighed, frustrated. She ended the call and slipped her phone back into her pocket. "No, he's *not* under the desk. He has a tendency to forget to take his cell phone with him."

"Like I said," Logan told her, starting to make his way over to the padded chair in the corner of the office, "I don't mind waiting."

"Waiting for what, young man?"

Andy and the man she's been verbally sparring with turned in unison to see Richard Roman standing in the hallway, less than half a foot shy of the office threshold.

CHAPTER FIVE

"WAITING FOR YOU, SIR," Logan replied to the older man's question. "I don't mind waiting for you," he said, stating the complete sentence so that the other man would understand. "If you're Richard Roman, that is," he qualified, although he was fairly certain that the man he was addressing was the same man he had been sent to speak with.

"I am," Richard replied. He looked from the stranger to his daughter and made a natural assumption. "Why don't you introduce me to your friend, Andy?"

"He's not my friend." The disclaimer shot across the room like a bullet when Andy bit the words out.

Crossing, Logan extended his right hand. "Pleased to meet you, Mr. Roman. I'm Logan MacArthur."

"Logan MacArthur," Richard repeated

as he returned the man's firm handshake. He rolled the name over in his mind and came up empty. It was unfamiliar to him. "To what do I owe this pleasure?"

"Don't jump to conclusions, Dad," Andy was quick to caution. "This might not be a pleasure in the long run." The warning left her father more puzzled than ever. He glanced quizzically at Logan.

"This won't take up too much of your time, sir," Logan promised, continuing as if Andy hadn't said a word. "If you don't mind, I'd like to speak to you privately."

Richard shrugged as he responded, "I don't see why not."

Andy's uneasiness refused to abate. Her protective instincts went up another notch. "Dad, maybe one of us should stay for this," she suggested.

"One of us is staying, Andy," her father pointed out with a touch of humor.

He knew what she meant, Andy thought, tamping down her exasperation. She was referring to herself and her sisters. It was hard protecting her father from whatever this man was up to if her own father was hindering her attempts to intervene.

"I meant one of us *besides* you, Dad," she clarified tersely.

"It's okay, Andy. Really," Richard assured her with a warm, patient smile. "I'll fill all of you in later." And with that, the door closed, leaving Andy standing there, frustrated and exasperated beyond words.

She remained there for a few moments, wondering if there was some way she could listen in on what was being said. Her father's health worried her and she didn't want him facing any upsetting news alone. It didn't matter that he'd been running the inn for a good many years, all that mattered was the immediate present and keeping her father healthy.

She didn't know if it was the mood she'd initially been in, or the vibrations she was getting from this MacArthur person, but there was no denying she had a bad feeling about this.

After a few more seconds had passed and neither her father nor MacArthur had come out, Andy began to believe she was overreacting. If whatever that annoying man had to tell her father was really important, her father would tell her.

He'd tell *all* of them, just as he'd promised. Just as he always did. Richard Roman was not a man who was given to hoarding secrets—although, Andy recalled as she walked back to the main reception area, her father *had* kept the matter of his health a secret all those years ago until he was almost too weak to stand. That heart trouble had been triggered from overwork.

His excuse had been that he hadn't wanted any of them to worry, she remembered, but that was exactly what happened when his health took a nosedive. Fearing the worst, they'd *all* worried.

Back then, fresh out of college, Alex had taken over, helming the inn and doing everything she could to keep it going until her father was well enough to get back to the job himself.

These days they were past rough patches like that, Andy thought, trying to find solace in that simple reality. These days the rough patches involved finding a way to be tactful when they had to turn guests away because the inn was booked up.

Not exactly a hardship. Andy smiled to herself. They had more business than they could handle and it was wonderful.

"Ah, if it isn't Miss Grumpy-pants," Alex declared as Andy walked into reception. "Did you take that gorgeous guy to Dad's office or will the San Diego county police department be bringing the cadaver dogs out to the inn in a couple of days?"

She scowled. "Nice, Alex. Very adult. Don't talk to me as if we were characters on some Saturday morning cartoon show. And, for the record, you were the one we used to call Grumpy-pants when we were kids. Not me…" She paused. "There's something about that guy I just don't trust."

"So they *will* be bringing in the cadaver dogs?" Alex asked innocently.

Andy blew out a breath. "No dogs. I brought him to Dad's office." Her tone told Alex just how much she hadn't wanted to run that particular errand.

Alex clearly wasn't satisfied. "And was Dad there?"

Andy didn't know why her sister was being so suspicious. She wasn't the one under this roof who deserved the third degree. She gave a monotone, honest accounting. "Not at that moment, but then he turned up a couple of minutes later."

"Then Mr. Gorgeous is still alive and breathing?"

Enough was enough. Just because the man was extremely attractive didn't automatically negate everything else and make him a good guy.

"You keep calling him that and I'm going to tell Wyatt you were drooling over some stranger."

"I'm not drooling, I'm paying attention. Besides, I'm married, not dead. I don't expect Wyatt not to take note of other women. He can browse through any catalogue he wants," she told Andy loftily. "As long as he doesn't place an order, it's okay with me."

That was a really strange way to put it. But then, Alex had never been known as the conventional sister. "And Wyatt, he shares this little philosophy of yours?"

"He does," Alex replied firmly, adding, "because he knows what's good for him." She punctuated her statement with a wide smile.

Andy just shook her head. Nothing was straightforward anymore. "It sounds way too complicated to me," she said. She absently glanced down at her unadorned left hand. "Maybe not being married isn't such a bad thing after all."

"Just wait, Andrea Roman. Your time will come."

The in-house line rang. Alex reached for the phone stored beneath the desk to make room for the ledger. "Hello?"

Andy was instantly alert. "Is it Dad?" she wanted to know. "Does he want to see me?"

Alex waved away both questions, concentrating on what was being said on the other end of the line.

"Yes, yes, of course. I'll send someone to you right away. And don't worry, I'll call a doctor. It's Dr. Donnelly. I've got his number right here. Hang on, help is on the way." Hanging up, Alex looked straight at her sister. "You're it," she declared.

Andy wasn't sure what had just happened or who Alex had been talking to. "As in tag?" she asked, bewildered.

Alex shook her head, her blond hair all but dancing around her face. "As in the help I promised."

Andy felt something tighten around her heart. "Dad?" Alex's earlier dismissal hadn't fully convinced her.

"Ms. Carlyle," Alex corrected. "I'd go myself but in my present shape, I don't exactly inspire confidence and I'm not exactly built for speed, so you're elected."

"Ms. Carlyle?" Andy repeated. It took a second for the name to get past her concern for her father. Another full second to fully register. "What's wrong with her?"

"Other than being in her late eighties, early nineties?"

No one really knew the woman's exact age. And Ms. Carlyle made it clear she preferred it that way. She had pointed out a long time ago that the inn's main objective was to make her stay with them as pleasant an experience as humanly possible. This automatically included allowing the woman to maintain both her secrets and her dignity if those secrets contributed to Ms. Carlyle's sense of dignity.

"Yes," Andy answered with as much patience as she could muster, "other than that."

"My guess is that it might be her heart," Alex speculated, going through the list of regularly used phone numbers to locate the doctor's. "She confided in Wyatt that she'd been having occasional…flutters…I think she called them."

The term, as far as Andy knew, covered a wide variety of complaints for the former elementary school teacher. "She's still sweet on Wyatt, huh?"

Alex nodded, still searching. "Ever since he interviewed her for that book his father had been writing about the inn. Here it is," she cried triumphantly, jabbing the number with her well-polished nail for emphasis. "I'll call the doctor, ask him to please come here and see her." She glanced up at Andy. "I just hope he's up to it. He's getting on in years, too." Alex sighed. "Things aren't supposed to keep changing like this," she lamented.

"If they didn't," Andy pointed out even though she didn't care for change, either, "you and Wyatt would still be exchanging barbs instead of making babies."

"Go!" Alex ordered, pointing in the direction of their only live-in guest's quarters. "You're wasting time. She could be freaking out."

The stately Ms. Anne Josephine Carlyle spent a good deal of her time in the Queen Mary Suite, one of the inn's original rooms. It was on the first floor within easy walking distance of the dining hall as well as the back veranda. The latter had an incredible view of the ocean and at night, during a full moon, it appeared as if the moon and the ocean were enjoying a secret relationship built on affection and gentle caresses.

Andy shook her head free of that image. She needed to get out more.

A second before she reached Ms. Carlyle's room, Andy caught movement out of the corner of her eye. Turning, she saw

MacArthur on his way to reception. She couldn't make out the expression on his face so she had no clue if his secret little meeting with her father had gone well or not. The second she was finished checking on Ms. Carlyle, she was going to check on her father. If he wasn't forthcoming about what had happened, she intended to nag him until she got the details.

She hated being out of the loop.

"Ms. Carlyle?" she called out as she knocked on the door a second time. "It's Andy, Ms. Carlyle. Alex sent me to check on you. I'm going to unlock your door if that's all right with you."

But as she began to reach for her key— her father refused to have the inn's doors changed to accommodate keycards—the door to the Queen Mary Suite opened. The petite, thin-boned woman stood like a queen in the doorway, barring access to her room.

"No, it is *not* all right with me," she declared in a clipped, no-nonsense voice that generations of fifth graders still had nightmares about. "If I allow you to waltz in

like that, then before you know it, everyone
will be coming in any time the whim over-
takes them. There goes my privacy, trampled in exchange for your convenience."
The glare on her shockingly smooth face
was the kind that put fear into the hearts
of stronger people than the one she was
facing.

Andy did a quick once-over of the for-
midable woman before her. "I guess you're
feeling okay, then. Thank goodness."

Ms. Carlyle snorted dismissively. "Another wrong assumption," she informed
Andy curtly. "I've been having these—
these flutters off and on for three hours
now."

Andy was immediately alert. This could
well be serious.

"Anything else?" Andy wanted to know,
her gaze never leaving Ms. Carlyle's.

The older woman's deep gray eyes narrowed. "Isn't that enough?"

Andy was quick when it came to damage
control and placating the former teacher.

"Yes, of course it's enough. More than
enough. But I just wanted to get everything

down so that we can give the doctor the information we have all at once so there's no question of omission."

But Ms. Carlyle had gotten stuck on a single pronoun. "We," she repeated. "Are you having flutters as well, Andrea?"

Too late, Andy realized her mistake. The woman was a stickler for grammar and for accuracy—even in dire situations.

"No," Andy replied with just a touch of contrition, hoping that would be enough for the former teacher.

But Ms. Carlyle was focused on exacting an apology. "I didn't think so. So then you agree that there is no 'we' in this situation." Her eyes never left Andy's face. "There is only me—and you," she allowed, "if you have any symptoms you'd like to report to the good doctor."

"Not today," Andy quickly told her. "Today is all about you. It's a lucky thing the doctor's willing to make house calls." She sure hoped he was on his way. Dr. Donnelly had put on some weight in the past year or so and moved with the speed of an aging turtle. But the man was good and he was accommodating. They would have been hard-pressed to find a doctor with a better bedside manner than Dr. Tom Donnelly.

Ms. Carlyle snorted dismissively, as if she didn't think a doctor who made house calls was such a big deal.

"When I was your age, Andrea," the older woman said, reminiscing as Andy gently guided her back into her room and toward her bed, "they *all* made house calls. It was expected. And they didn't charge an arm and a leg for it, either."

She slowly lowered herself onto her bed, deliberately avoiding Andy's help.

"In those days, people became doctors because they wanted to help people, not because they wanted to get rich and retire early to hit a silly little dimpled ball around with different fancy sticks."

Andy smiled, trying to be as supportive as she could. Ms. Carlyle was a prickly bill of goods when she wanted to be, and one never knew what might set the woman off and what might actually appeal to her.

When they did find the latter, it usually

only lasted for a moment, but it was something to strive for as far as she and her sisters were concerned.

"The good old days," Andy confirmed agreeably.

Ms. Carlyle gave her a penetrating look to see if she was being mocked.

Apparently satisfied that she wasn't, she replied, "Yes, they were, and don't you forget it. Well, are you just going to hover around my room like some lost wraith or are you going to sit down like a civilized young woman with a smattering of manners?"

"I'd like to sit down if it's all right with you," Andy answered, indicating the chair in the corner near the bed.

"I wouldn't have asked you if you were going to sit down if I didn't want you to," Ms. Carlyle pointed out in exasperation. "Really, child, how does your poor father put up with you?"

"He manages," Andy replied quietly.

There were times, such as now, that Ms. Carlyle played the part of the disgruntled old woman so well it was hard for Andy to figure out the line between reality and playacting.

Or if there even was a separation.

For all she knew, the woman really was like this, just plain ornery to the very core. If there was a moment's deviation, that's all it was, a temporary deviation. The woman would be back to her salty self in a moment or two.

Andy noticed that she was sitting on her bed, ramrod straight. To have posture like that at her age was beyond remarkable. "Maybe you should lie down," Andy suggested.

But again, Ms. Carlyle saw things differently. "There'll be plenty of time for that when I'm dead," she assured Andy. "Besides, the flutters get worse when I lie down." Her own words caused the former teacher to look even more dismayed. "You don't think I'm going to have to sleep sitting up for the rest of my life, do you?"

"Don't go borrowing trouble, Ms. Carlyle," Andy told the woman gently, espousing the philosophy that her sisters and she had been taught since they were very young. "If it turns out to be true, well, there's nothing you could have done about it. But if it turns out not to be the case, then you have wasted all that time, feeling sorry for yourself when you didn't have to. In the end, thinking the worst is just a terrible waste of time."

She saw Ms. Carlyle open her mouth to offer a rebuttal, but instead, she abruptly closed it again, as if she was giving that some thought.

Had she actually gotten through to the woman, or was she being set up, Andy couldn't help wondering.

Her speculation was cut short by a knock on the door.

Andy brightened. "That has to be the doctor," she told the older woman. "I'll get it."

"That's what you're here for," Ms Carlyle reminded her crisply.

Andy swung open the door to let in Dr. Donnelly.

But the tall, dark, handsome man standing in the doorway was definitely not a man approaching the eighth decade of his life.

Definitely not Dr. Donnelly.

CHAPTER SIX

"HI, I'M DR. DONNELLY." Andy took in the warm smile, crisp, new black medical bag and the dark gray three-piece suit.

She couldn't help noticing that his gray-blue shirt intensified the color of his eyes, making them almost hypnotic.

"No, you're not." It seemed to be a day for arguing, she thought wearily. "I've known Dr. Tom Donnelly all my life. He's not much taller than I am, has a wonderful bedside manner and looks a little like Santa Claus. And you are definitely *not* him."

"No," he agreed. "I'm not." The man in the hallway shifted his medical bag to his other hand and dug into his jacket's inside breast pocket. Extracting his wallet, he flipped it open to reveal his driver's license.

"You're talking about my uncle Tom,"

he told her, holding up his license for her perusal. "I'm Dr. Ryan Donnelly. I joined his practice early this June. My father— his younger brother—thinks Uncle Tom is working too hard and neglecting his health. Quite frankly, the family's worried about him."

Andy could see that Ms. Carlyle was less than pleased with this turn of events. "Does that mean that I won't be seeing Dr. Tom anymore?" The query sounded more like a challenge than a question.

"Oh, no. Uncle Tom is still practicing medicine," the younger Dr. Donnelly was quick to assure his new patient, crossing to her bed. "But he's only seeing patients in his office—or the local hospital. He won't be making any more house calls."

He smiled at the crotchety former school teacher as he gently took her wrist to note the rhythm of her heartbeat.

"But he didn't want to leave his house-bound patients high and dry. Knowing how stubborn Uncle Tom can be and how dedicated he is, the only way we knew to make him cut back his workload was if I said that I'd take over the house calls for him. So I did."

Ms. Carlyle snorted. "Practicing medicine indeed. You'd think after all this time, the man wouldn't have to practice. He should have gotten it right by now." Her sharp eyes narrowed as she gave this new Dr. Donnelly a penetrating, very slow once-over. "How old are you, boy? Fifteen?"

"Older," Ryan told her, amused rather than insulted. His easygoing reaction went a long way in winning Andy over. "I assure you that I have a degree in internal medicine."

"Where's it from? A correspondence school?" Ms. Carlyle challenged.

"I think she might mean online," Andy interjected helpfully.

Ms. Carlyle shot her a withering look. "Don't speak for me, girl. I know exactly what I mean. Mail-in school," she repeated.

"I have a degree from the USC Keck School of Medicine," the doctor told her, putting her hand back down on her lap and opening his bag. "Do you have any other questions for me?"

"Yes," Ms. Carlyle declared with a sharp nod of her head. And then she shrugged. "But they can wait. My heart keeps fluttering—and before you make some kind of silly remark, it's not because you're so good-looking," she snapped. "Even if you are."

"I wouldn't dream of making a silly remark at your expense, Ms. Carlyle," he told her with sincerity, taking out a stethoscope as well as several other basic instruments. "Now, I'll need to examine you."

"What about her?" Ms. Carlyle wanted to know, nodding at Andy.

"What about her?" Dr. Donnelly asked, his tone far milder than his patient's had been.

"Is she supposed to stand there, staring like that while you poke and prod me?" Ms. Carlyle demanded.

Ryan slanted a glance at the young woman who had answered the door just now, then looked back to his patient.

"Only if you want her to. I want you to

be perfectly comfortable, Ms. Carlyle," he said in a low, soothing voice that, at another time and place, might have been employed to calm down an agitated child. It was part of his bedside manner, and for the most part it worked, putting his patients at ease.

His answer—which for all intents and purposes placed the power in her hands—seemed to satisfy the older woman. She shook her head ever so slightly. "No need for a chaperone," she told him. "Handsome man like you must have his share of young women to choose from. I doubt very much if your taste would stray to an old woman like me."

"Age, Ms. Carlyle," he said, walking over to the small bathroom, "is just a number."

Preparing to do a quick examination—although he had his suspicions as to what was ailing the woman—Ryan turned the water on and quickly washed his hands.

"And mine is a large one," Ms. Carlyle replied. But the older woman appeared to be rather pleased by the doctor's philosophy. Turning to Andy, she waved the younger woman on her way. "You can go do whatever it was you were doing, Andrea. The boy doctor and I will take it from here."

Andy wasn't about to argue with the woman. Ms. Carlyle rarely changed her mind once she'd made it up. "Just call the front desk if you need me."

Her remark was actually intended for both parties since she felt that the doctor might have some instructions for Ms. Carlyle that he wanted to go over with her. Since the woman had no family—at least, none she had ever mentioned—the sisters and her father were it.

Having said what she needed to and feeling that she was leaving Ms. Carlyle in good hands, Andy turned on her heel and left the room.

When she returned to the reception desk some fifteen minutes later, after having talked with several guests who had stopped her to ask a few questions about tourist attractions in the area, she found that Alex was still perched on her stool.

Her oldest sister was in the middle of

reviewing next month's reservations but the moment she saw Andy approaching, Alex put everything else on hold. Ms. Carlyle was not given to dramatics where her health was involved. In that regard, the older woman liked to display an air of invincibility. That she had asked for a doctor was disturbing. Her flutters had never driven her to seek medical help before this.

"So?" Alex asked, a huge question mark hanging in the air beside the single, one-syllable word. "How is she?"

Andy didn't answer her directly. She had a question of her own first. "Did you know that Dr. Donnelly had a nephew?"

Alex's eyebrows drew together quizzically beneath her bangs. "You mean that young doctor who came through here who shares the same last name? Well, it occurred to me they might be related. I saw him a couple of times at the clinic, and had seen the second Donnelly name posted under Dr. Tom's on the front door. In such a small town, they had to be related, but nephew, huh? Interesting."

A troubling thought must have suddenly occurred to her.

"He hasn't retired, has he?" Alex asked, clearly concerned at the prospect. "Dr. Tom?"

"No, he's still practicing medicine according to what his nephew told me in Ms. Carlyle's room." She looked at Alex more closely. Her sister appeared genuinely upset. "Why?"

"Because I've been going to Dr. Donnelly all my life, so of course I went to him for my prenatal exams," Alex told her, lowering her voice even though none of the inn's guests were anywhere within earshot. "I wanted him to deliver my baby, not some guy who looks like he just stepped off the cover of a fashion magazine."

That was definitely a fitting description of the new doctor, Andy thought. "Then you've met the guy."

"Of course I've met him," Alex confirmed impatiently. "Who do you think gave him directions on how to find Ms. Carlyle's room?" Alex was chewing on her lower lip, a sure sign that she was upset and struggling not to look that way. "You sure our Dr. Donnelly hasn't retired?"

Andy smiled. "I'm sure." She understood exactly how her sister felt. But she still couldn't pass up the opportunity to tease Alex. "A doctor's a doctor, Alex. They all took the same oath to do no harm."

"Maybe so," Alex allowed, "but I want one who's been in the trenches for a while now, not one who's probably doing every procedure for the very first time."

Amused, Andy told her oldest sister, "Even God had a first day."

"Maybe," Alex said for the sake of argument, "but it didn't involve an up close and personal exam," she retorted. "You know, Andy—"

She had teased Alex long enough, Andy decided. She held her hands up in the universal sign of surrender. "Uncle," she cried, trying to look solemn and failing miserably.

"Uncle?" Alex repeated, clearly somewhat bewildered.

"As in I give up, not as in Young Doctor Kildare's uncle."

"Dr. Kildare?" Alex echoed, still very much in the dark.

"Never mind."

Clearly the obscure movie references she'd picked up after dating a film student and sitting through three months of classic films every Friday night was wasted on her sister.

"I was just teasing you." She saw the displeased expression on Alex's face. "You know, you never had all that much of a sense of humor to begin with, Alex. But ever since you've gotten pregnant, you just have no sense of humor at all. See? If the grumpy-pants fit…"

"You try lugging around thirty-two extra pounds everywhere you go and see how much of *your* sense of humor remains intact," Alex challenged her.

"Cris seems to manage," Andy pointed out. "And this is her second time around. She's dealing with a brand-new husband, a slightly used first grader, running the kitchen and a pregnancy."

Andy couldn't resist the poke. She knew Alex had never cared for being compared to anyone else and especially coming in second. That the comparison was to one of her own sisters would just make things worse in her eyes.

"Cris isn't real, she's an android," Alex said dismissively. "Now, if all you intend to do is hang around here and irritate me, why don't you go see if you can make your-self useful to Cris."

"Sure you don't want me to hunt for your missing sense of humor?" Andy inquired.

"Just get out of here," Alex ordered, pointing in the general direction of the kitchen.

"Your wish is my command," Andy said, turning on her heel.

"If only..." she heard Alex say under her breath as she left reception.

Andy needed to look in on her father first. The mysterious, closemouthed law-yer had left the inn a while ago and Andy had to admit that her curiosity had kicked into high gear.

It was probably nothing, Andy told her-self, but until she knew for sure, her imagination was going to keep conjuring up less-than-comforting scenarios.

So instead of turning left and going through the dining area to the kitchen, Andy continued walking straight, heading toward the back of the inn. She made a sharp right just before she reached the back entrance and the wraparound veranda that encompassed most of the inn just outside the double doors.

When she reached it, the door to her father's small office was closed. She couldn't tell if he was inside or if he'd gone to see to the myriad of small details that went into running the inn so smoothly.

Curbing her desire to just walk in, Andy knocked. When she received no response, she knocked again, this time a little harder.

"Dad, it's Andy, your favorite," she tossed in whimsically, appealing to his sense of humor. "Are you in there?"

At this point, she didn't think that he was—after all, he wasn't answering—but nonetheless her curiosity was growing by leaps and bounds. It had already almost gotten the better of her.

She debated her course of action for exactly ten seconds. Her father might not be in, but the annoying Logan MacArthur might have given him something from his briefcase. Legal papers, for instance.

If he had, and those papers were somewhere on her father's desk, she could at least satisfy the nagging concerns that were tying her stomach up in knots.

Andy checked to either side to make sure that there was no one in the hallway. Especially not Dorothy, Silvio or a family member.

There was no one and nothing around, except for her own conscience.

She disregarded it.

Andy opened the door ever so slowly, taking care not to allow it to squeak, and stepped inside. She was so intent on being soundless, she didn't realize until after a couple of seconds had passed that her father was still in the room, at his desk. She only noticed after she'd eased the door closed again.

Andy stifled a gasp. Her father's chair was turned away from his desk and was facing the window, which was why she hadn't realized he was in the room.

Drawing air into her lungs to calm her jangled nerves, she blew out the breath before speaking.

"Dad," she began, addressing the back of his head, "why didn't you answer when I knocked?"

Her father remained where he was, facing the window, saying nothing.

That made her uneasy.

Her father didn't believe in the silent treatment. Nor did he ever express any sort of anger, no matter what she or her sisters might have been guilty of doing. That just wasn't his way.

Her father believed in talking things out, in getting to the bottom of things and working with the guilty party to smooth things over.

Still, she had this small, nagging fear that MacArthur had said something to her father about her less-than-professional behavior that might have embarrassed her father and now he was annoyed with her.

She realized that she could put up with anything, except having him upset with her.

"Dad?" Andy tried again, talking to the back of his head. "Are you angry with me? Whatever that idiot in the expensive suit told you, I was just trying to find out what he wanted from you. I was trying to protect you because you've got more than enough on your plate and I didn't want you worrying about anything extra."

More silence.

Her father didn't even make an attempt to turn around and look at her.

That wasn't like him.

This wasn't right, Andy thought. Her father just didn't behave this way.

"Dad?" she said, louder now as she moved forward. "Are you all right?"

He made no answer.

"Talk to me, Dad."

Standing in front of her father, Andy first wondered if he might have fallen asleep. All in all, that wasn't such a rare occurrence. Added to that, it was a rather overcast day, the kind they rarely had out here except during the rainy season. And she knew for a fact that her father had been working on inventory last night.

Maybe work had finally caught up with him. The lawyer had probably bored him to sleep and, after he'd left, her father had just decided to get in a few minutes of shut-eye.

A cat nap, so to speak.

Why didn't she believe that? Andy was growing more nervous.

She put her hand on top of her father's. She felt what she took to be a disconcerting dampness along the top of his.

Holding her breath, Andy slipped her fingers around his wrist to gauge his pulse.

It was beating erratically: quickly, then skipping beats before beating quickly again.

Something was very wrong.

"Dad?" she tried one last time. "Dad, please talk to me!"

All she received in response was the sound of labored breathing. Why hadn't she heard that when she'd first stepped in? What was wrong with her?

Her mind scrambled, scattering in all

different directions, and for a second she was too paralyzed to take any sort of action, reasonable or otherwise.

The next moment Andy was racing back down the hallway to the reception desk.

"Alex," she shouted, "call Ms. Carlyle's room. I need the doctor."

"So, you're finally deciding not to play hard to get, is that it?"

Andy came to a skidding halt, utterly bewildered by what Alex was saying to her. And then it hit her.

"No, not for me," she cried. "It's for Dad!" When Alex still didn't seem to understand her, Andy yelled, "I can't wake him up! We need the doctor. I think Dad needs help."

Alex stared at her in utter dismay as her words finally sank in.

"Oh, Andy, Dr. Donnelly left about two, three minutes ago!"

But Andy was already gone, shooting across the front lobby, setting what was probably a new record.

Pushing the front doors wide open with

the flat of her hands, she sprinted to the parking lot, searching for an unfamiliar car.

Searching for the doctor.

CHAPTER SEVEN

ANDY DIDN'T HAVE a clue what kind of vehicle this new Dr. Donnelly would drive so she didn't know what make or model car she was looking for.

A quick scan of the area told her that he wasn't driving his uncle's car.

The old Dr. Donnelly favored an original, faded-orange VW Bug. Because of its style and the attention-grabbing color, it was easy to spot anywhere, even in a crowded parking lot.

The inn's main parking lot was half-filled.

Andy's stomach sank. Had the doctor left already?

In that case, she should be calling 911 instead of wasting time, she thought urgently.

Out of the corner of her eye she caught a movement. A white Toyota Camry with several years and dings on it was backing out of its spot.

Hoping against hope that this was the doctor's car, Andy made a mad dash to it. She arrived just in time to place herself in front of the dusty vehicle as the driver switched from Reverse to Drive.

In her anxious state, she'd cut it just a wee bit too close and had to quickly back up. Otherwise, she would have become its brand-new hood ornament.

Startled to have a woman jump out of nowhere directly in front of his vehicle, Ryan Donnelly slammed on his brakes, which in turn whined loudly in protest.

At the same time, he swerved to the left, avoiding the young woman he had met earlier by inches.

"Do you have a death wish?" he shouted out of his window as he uncoupled his seatbelt.

Ryan was really shaken up by how close he had come to hitting her. He was in the business of saving lives, not taking them.

Andy didn't bother answering his question. Instead, the second he was out of the vehicle she grabbed his arm and propelled him toward the inn again. Expecting not to be budged, Ryan was rather amazed at the amount of strength this woman exhibited. She certainly was a lot stronger than she appeared.

"You have to come back," Andy insisted frantically, dragging him in her wake.

The doctor stared at her as if she had just lost her mind.

"I just left Ms. Carlyle, and aside from a mild form of A-fib, she seemed fine. Actually, she seemed to be in better condition than some of my other patients. Did something else happen to her?"

He couldn't have left her more than three minutes ago.

Andy shook her head emphatically. "This isn't about Ms. Carlyle," she cried. "It's my father. I think he's had a heart attack. He's unconscious and I couldn't get him to respond."

Ryan immediately picked up his pace, no longer running behind the young woman who was still holding on to his arm, but next to her.

"When did this happen?"

"Sometime in the last half hour," she estimated. That was when she'd seen that lawyer leaving the inn. "I just went in to check on him," Andy told the doctor, struggling to get control over her mounting panic.

He's going to be all right. Dad's going to be all right.

"This way!" she declared as she and Ryan bust into the inn.

Alex wasn't at reception and neither was anyone else. She had to have gone to their father's office, Andy guessed.

When they reached him a couple of minutes later, she saw that not only was Alex there but so were her other sisters as well as Dorothy and Silvio. There was barely any room in the tiny office to turn around.

The four women were gathered around her father while Silvio was checking his vital signs.

"There is a pulse," the gardener said. "It is weak, but now stronger than it was a few minutes before."

"Are you a doctor?" Ryan asked the short, dark-haired man for his own edification.

"He was in his country," Stevi answered, stepping in to handle the matter for the man who had so recently saved her fiancé's life. There were many things that Silvio had been in his country that were better left unsaid. A doctor had been the most honorable of his vocations.

Ryan quickly assessed the situation. Ideally, he wanted to clear the room, but for now, he settled for some space.

"I need a little room here," Ryan requested. Andy's sisters huddled together, doing what they could to comply with the doctor's request while still remaining in the room. "Is this his first episode?" he wanted to know, throwing the question out for any one of them to answer.

Alex took the lead, just as she had the first time all those years ago. "The first one that we know of…recently," Alex qualified. "He doesn't like to worry us. Dad had a minor episode about eight years ago. Angina," she supplied when the doctor raised an eyebrow.

"Dr. Donnelly—your uncle—had him hospitalized for a couple of days and then placed him on restricted activity for a couple of months. But he's been frail recently—and we're concerned."

It was during that time that Alex had taken over running the inn, that she'd discovered she had both a flair for it and a taste for it. It had changed her mind-set about what she was going to do with the rest of her life.

"Is he going to be all right?" Alex asked, giving voice to the one question that was on all of their minds.

"He should be," Ryan replied.

"'Should be?'" Andy questioned sharply.

"I need more input before I can give you a definite maybe," Ryan answered, his attention focused on his patient.

Dr. Donnelly took their father's temperature, his blood pressure and performed a few cursory tests. It was while he was shining a light into his eyes, that Richard regained consciousness.

Blinking to shut out the light that was all but blinding him, Richard squinted as he looked up at the man working over him. A bewildered expression slipping over his gaunt face.

"Who are you?" Richard asked, blinking.

"This is Dr. Ryan Donnelly, Dad. He's Dr. Tom's nephew," Alex explained.

A huge sigh of relief escaped Andy's lips. Their father was conscious. He was going to be all right.

"You gave us all quite a scare, Dad," Alex said.

Richard Roman had never liked being the center of attention. Even when he was a child, growing up at the inn, adorable in the eyes of many of the guests. He hadn't liked it then; he didn't like it now.

He liked being the center of concern even less.

Deliberately masking his confusion by putting on an innocent expression, Richard asked defensively, "Can't a man take a nap in his office without setting off some sort of a chain reaction?"

Ryan hadn't finished his exam yet, but some things were already apparent. "You weren't napping, Mr. Roman. My preliminary diagnosis is that you had an anxiety attack."

"So it wasn't a heart attack, Doctor?" Andy asked.

"Let's just say that his heart hiccupped," he told Andy. "I want to conduct a more thorough examination, but I can already see that I'm going to have to prescribe a medication for you. Do you use the pharmacy in town?" he asked Richard.

Richard in turn looked at Alex, who handled those sorts of details. "Do I?"

Alex smiled at her father, taking this to be a good sign that things were going to return to normal very soon. She rattled off the phone number she knew by heart. "Anything else, doctor?" she asked.

"Yes, call our office and schedule a follow-up for your father. I'd like to run a few tests on him to make sure there's nothing else going on with your dad that we should know about."

"Absolutely," Alex guaranteed. "I'll call as soon as I get back to the front desk."

"Maybe you should admit Dad to the

hospital," Cris suggested. "You know, just to be certain everything's all right."

"I like to keep people *out* of the hospital if at all possible," Ryan said, surprising them all. "Hospitals are a hotbed of a lot of different diseases and I don't want your father catching something while he's being seen for chest pains."

He looked thoughtfully at Richard. He had a little time on his hands and he could see that the man's daughters were desperate for reassurance that this was just a minor incident.

"If you ladies don't mind, I'd like to conduct a more thorough examination of my patient," he proposed.

"Why did you just change your mind?" Andy asked.

"Because I'm human," he replied with a smile. "This way, if I conduct an extended examination, you can be reassured about your father's health."

"And that's the only reason?" she asked, her eyes boring into his.

"That's the only reason," he told her in all seriousness.

Everyone filed out. Andy was the last to go, lingering only long enough to take the business card she saw on her father's desk.

The one with Logan MacArthur's name on it.

Pocketing the card discreetly, Andy filed out behind her sisters.

Everyone remained in the hall, gathering a few feet away from the room they had left, waiting to see if there was anything further to learn about Richard Roman's condition. The mood was not nearly as tense as it had been a few minutes ago. For the most part, they felt that, at least for now, the worst was over.

But while the others opted to remain close by, Andy just kept walking. Determined.

"Andy," Alex called after her. "Where are you going?"

Andy saw no reason to lie or make up an excuse. "I'm going to find out what that lawyer said to Dad to give him a heart attack."

"Andy, the doctor said it was an anxiety attack, not a heart attack," Cris called.

"He left it open to interpretation—and it was still an attack," Andy tossed over her shoulder as she kept walking. "I want that rat to come clean." She turned down the hall.

Concerned, Stevi caught up with her just shy of the front doors.

She caught Andy by the shoulders to get her attention—and to hold her in place for a minute.

"Andy, Dad's going to need us here. Don't go off half-cocked," she warned.

Andy shrugged Stevi off. "I'm not half-cocked. I'm fully cocked and ready to go off if that so-and-so doesn't answer my questions."

Stevi knew that there was no stopping Andy when she was like this. All she could do was make a request and hope that Andy would honor it.

"Please, don't do anything without talking to us first. Most of all, don't do anything stupid."

"I'm not the one who did something stupid," Andy informed her sister. Her voice was tinged with barely controlled anger.

And then she was gone.

GLANCING ONCE AT the address on the card Logan MacArthur had left on her father's desk, Andy gunned her twelve-year-old hand-me-down vehicle and took off.

With one eye on the rearview mirror, watching for the telltale signs of police, Andy flew through traffic lights, some of which were in the process of turning red.

She managed to make it to the address on the card in record time—if anyone was keeping track of such things.

Andy didn't remember getting out of her car. Right now, there was only one thing on her mind—if she didn't count getting her hands around the lawyer's throat and strangling him. She wanted to find out what the man had said to upset her father this way.

And she wanted the lawyer to know just what he had done. She doubted the man would apologize, but she wanted him to feel some sort of guilt for what he had caused.

Logan MacArthur's firm was located on the second floor of a fairly new five-story building that was all futuristic looking tinted glass and steel.

Andy didn't bother with the elevator, she took the stairs, two at a time, as she dashed up to the second floor.

When she emerged from the stairwell, she found that the firm was three doors down.

Andy swung open the office door and with quick, confident steps crossed to the front desk. "Which way to Logan MacArthur's office?"

"It's 2C, but you can't go in there," the receptionist said, raising her voice in alarm as Andy swept right by her.

In an instant, the woman was on her feet.

"Watch me," Andy shot over her shoulder just before she breeched the lawyer's inner sanctum.

Logan was sitting at his desk, dictating the notes from his last meeting into the software program that would eventually type the report up for him.

"It appears that this is not going to go down without incident—" Logan stopped midsentence as his office door slammed against the opposite wall. Richard Roman's uncooperative daughter stormed in

and resoundingly banged the door shut behind her.

Before Logan could ask her what she
was doing here and why she was shaking his office apart, Andy beat him to the
punch.

"What did you say to him?" Andy demanded, making it from the door to his
desk in what seemed like two giant leaps.

"Him?" Logan repeated, bewildered.

He'd recognized her immediately as the
woman who had given him so much attitude earlier at the inn, but he had no idea
why she would be this angry and incensed.
Or why she was phrasing her question the
way she was, if she knew his true position
in all this.

Damn it, Andy thought impatiently, he
was playing dumb. Did he think she was
stupid?

"My father," Andy spat out. "What did
you say to him?"

The dismayed receptionist hurried in
right behind Andy, clearly a little frightened. "Do you want me to call security, Mr.
MacArthur? They can have her removed

quickly," she said, as if she was giving him information that he hadn't heard dozens of times.

Logan was already on his feet. He rounded his desk, thinking he needed to calm Roman's daughter before she did something drastic. The matter of his own safety never even occurred to him.

"No need, Lisa. I can take care of this myself," he assured the flustered assistant. She nodded and backed out, hardly convinced.

"You mean like you took care of my father?" Andy retorted.

Now that they were alone again, Logan looked at her as if she were a puzzle come to life. "What are you talking about?"

"Okay, I'll put this is terms even you should be able to understand. Whatever you said to my father gave him an anxiety attack and he passed out. If I hadn't found him when I did, who knows? I might be planning my father's funeral service right now."

The lawyer seemed genuinely appalled by what she'd just said, but she chalked it up to his being a classic, slimy, opportunistic shyster, hoping to get her to lower her guard.

It wasn't going to happen. The man had a great deal to learn about the Roman sisters.

Logan was still grappling with what she'd told him. The look in his eyes was nothing if not leery. "Then he's not—?"

"Dead?" Andy supplied cynically. "No, no thanks to you. There was a doctor on the premises and he got to Dad just in time. Now, for the last time, *what did you say to him*?" She fairly shouted the question into his face.

Given the circumstances, Logan made a judgment call and decided that Roman's family would find out about this soon enough. There was no longer a need for secrecy now that he'd taken the first step with Richard.

"I told him that my firm was acting on behalf of the State of California. They wanted to buy the inn and we were prepared to offer your father the going rate for his property."

Stunned, Andy looked at the man as if

he had just declared that he was a tourist from Mars. "You want to buy Ladera by the Sea?" she asked, trying to get that straight in her head.

It took him a moment to remember that that was the name of the inn.

"The state does," he corrected her.

Her father, Andy knew, would never sell the inn. The inn was like another member of the family to him.

It would be like asking him to sell one of his daughters.

"The inn is not for sale," Andy informed the lawyer crisply.

"I'm afraid it has to be," Logan contradicted in a calm voice that was making Andy crazy. "I just don't want to make this unpleasant."

"Too late," she told him coldly. "And not that there's a chance Dad would ever consider changing his mind and sell you the inn, but exactly why do you think it 'has to be'?" she asked, quoting the phrase he'd just used.

"Because if your father doesn't agree to sell it to my client, my client—the state—

is going to come in, declare your property to be subject to eminent domain and take it from him. Compensation at that point plummets to ten cents on the dollar. When everything is said and done, quite bluntly, your father will lose the inn and every dime he ever put into it," Logan calmly informed the speechless woman standing before him.

CHAPTER EIGHT

THIS WAS COMPLETELY UNORTHODOX. Logan could only assume that the woman standing in front of him, her eyes blazing, was motivated by filial loyalty.

He was familiar with the concept, of course, even if he had never experienced the emotion firsthand. Love and loyalty hadn't been part of his formative years.

Or any of the years that came after.

Oh, growing up he'd never wanted for anything. His creature comforts had all been taken care of. He'd had the best of everything during those all-important formative years.

But he had never been privy to expressions of love or pride. His parents were both well-known in their fields. They devoted a great deal of time and effort to maintaining their positions—his dad as a big-business CEO and his mother as a charity fund-raiser. In short, they were decent people, but not loving. And they should have never procreated.

Decorum was of paramount importance to the senior members of the firm, so Logan did his best to calm the woman, who looked as if she'd start breathing fire at any moment.

"Hey, I'm not the bad guy here—" Logan began, only to be summarily cut off.

"You certainly could have fooled me," Andy retorted angrily.

Logan tried again, thinking that giving her an accounting of what had transpired—and why—would do the trick.

"I told your father I wanted him to have all the facts in front of him and that I would delay getting back to the firm's client, giving him time to think the offer over. Quite honestly, I thought that would buy your father a little time so that he could come around."

"Why does the state want the land? What does it want to develop it into?" Andy asked.

"That's between your father and the state, but if you're a fan of the arts I can tell you you won't be disappointed."

He could whitewash this all he wanted, Andy frowned to herself, but that didn't change the events—or their consequences. "What you told him, in effect, was that if he didn't come around and sell the inn, he'd lose everything. What you don't seem to understand," Andy accused him, struggling not to shout at the lawyer, "is that the inn *is* everything to him. It's been in our family for over a hundred and twenty years. He's lived and worked at the inn his entire life. My sisters and I have never known any other home except the inn. You can't be expected to put a price tag on that."

Logan refrained from saying that in his experience, everything had a price tag. Instead, he attempted to be diplomatic.

"I understand all that and I'm not unsympathetic," he told her, although quite frankly he really didn't understand being so attached to anything, especially an inanimate object like a building. "But the government will have its way," he continued, "and it would be best for your father if he accepted that."

"You don't get it, do you?" she asked, shaking her head.

Rather than the anger that had brought her here, she felt pity for the lawyer now. He hadn't a clue what went on in her father's mind, which meant that he himself had never felt that way about anything. She found that overwhelmingly sad.

"I guess we'll see you in court," Andy told him as she started to leave.

Logan stared at her incredulously. "You're actually going to fight this?" Had she not heard that the state was willing to spend quite a large sum of money for this acquisition?

Besides, this was a fight that was doomed from the very start. Against the state of California. She looked smart enough to know that.

This was what happened when people allowed their emotions to get in the way of their common sense.

"With every collective fiber of our being," she tossed over her shoulder as she took hold of the doorknob. She suddenly needed some fresh air.

"How's your father?"

The question stopped her dead in her tracks. Pausing, she said, "Not about to roll over and play dead." And with that, she slammed the door in her wake.

LIVID BEYOND WORDS, Andy didn't remember getting into her car, or even how she got down to the parking lot in the first place. It was all a blur.

She hardly remembered the trip home, either.

All she was aware of was her unbridled anger. That and the fact that they were going to need a lawyer, a darn good one who knew how to put obstacles in the government's way until they could figure out some final course of action to take to keep the inn.

Because, as she had told Logan MacArthur, it wasn't just an inn. It was also the only home she'd ever known and as such it was very precious to her.

As it was to the rest of her family.

There had to be a way to keep it.

"Where did you disappear to?" Alex asked her the second she walked through the inn's entrance.

Since several guests were milling around reception, admiring the Christmas tree, Andy crossed to her sister before she answered in a low voice, "Didn't Stevi tell you? I went to see that lawyer who caused Dad's anxiety attack."

"Andy, you didn't," Alex cried, appalled.

"Of course I did," Andy said.

"And?" Alex asked, prodding her to give up more information. "What did he say?"

Andy was torn between telling her sister about the state's so-called offer, and keeping it to herself until she could come up with some way to get the government to go away.

Both Alex and Cris were reaching the end of their respective pregnancies and she didn't want anything to upset them. She had no idea how this kind of news might affect their conditions. She knew it certainly affected hers, and she wasn't pregnant.

But if she kept this horrible news to herself and her sisters found out, they would be furious with her.

There was just no winning in this, Andy thought with a sigh, hoping that wasn't a sign of things to come.

"MacArthur represents a buyer and he approached Dad about selling the inn," she told Alex as matter-of-factly as she could while still keeping the details vague.

"Sell the inn?" Alex repeated, staring at her as if she was crazy. "You're kidding."

"Do I look like I'm kidding?" she shot back before she managed to get her temper under control.

She sincerely wished she was kidding.

Alex placed her hand over her heart.

"No, you don't." She frowned. "All Dad had to do was say no, thanks. I don't see why that would have triggered a myocardial infarction."

Alex studied her suspiciously.

"There has to be more to it," she insisted.

After a moment of internal debate, Andy replied, "There is." She waited until the inn's guests had all moved on to the dining area.

Andy looked at her sister, wondering if there was some good way to present this next piece of information and decided that there wasn't. She might as well spit it out.

"MacArthur also said that the buyer is the State of California."

"The state wants our land?" Alex echoed. Her brow furrowed as she tried to make sense of what Andy had just said. For now, she couldn't. "What does the state want with our inn?"

"They don't want anything…" Andy answered bluntly "…except to hit it dead-on with a wrecking ball."

"What?" Alex cried, her eyes widening. Another guest had just come down the stairs and paused to glance back at the two sisters as she was about to enter the dining room.

The pair pretended to busy themselves over the register until the guest went through the door.

Andy blew out a breath, struggling for control. "You heard me," she said, keeping her voice low. "In a nutshell, the state wants the land the inn is standing on."

"Well, they can't have it," Alex declared defiantly, her anger a clear match for her sister's.

"Apparently, according to that lawyer, it's not so simple," Andy said, fervently wishing it was.

"I know," Alex snapped, frustrated. "But we can—and will—fight them every step of the way. There has to be *something* we can do. Wyatt can get that lawyer friend of his to help," she said, thinking out loud. "You know, the one he brought in when we thought Cris's in-laws were going to get custody of Ricky."

Andy nodded, remembering the whole incident vividly. In the end it turned out that Cris didn't need the lawyer's services, but it had been touch-and-go for a while.

"And if he can't help, he'll know someone who can," Alex reasoned.

"Have Wyatt call him," Andy told her. "The more people we get on our side, the better."

"Are you thinking of staging a demonstration?" Alex wanted to know.

"I'm thinking of anything and everything that'll impede the state from taking our inn," Andy declared fiercely.

"Don't you think that Dad should be the one in charge of this?"

Andy shook her head. "He's already dealing with enough. First we come up with a viable plan of action, then we present it to him for a final okay. I don't want him getting any more upset than he is."

"I'll call Wyatt and tell him what's going on." Alex's voice rose and melted into a squeak unexpectedly at the end of her sentence. Andy's attention immediately shifted from the inn to her sister.

"Alex?" She peered at her. "Is something wrong?"

"Nothing," Alex snapped.

"'Nothing' is causing you to make weird noises," Andy pointed out. There was only one thing that she knew of that could do that. "Is it the baby?" At this point, the question was rhetorical.

Alex responded with a vague half shrug. "It's getting restless," she admitted.

Andy knew Alex better than she knew herself. Her sister was determined not to behave any differently than she normally did. Childbirth was, after all, just part of life, right? That's what Alex was trying to make herself think, and it was quite simply ridiculous.

"You should see the doctor, too—just in case," Andy suggested. "Is he still here?"

Alex shook her head. "He left about five minutes before you got back."

The threat of losing the inn had made her forget what was really important here. "With Dad?"

"No, Dad's still here. The doctor got him to agree to stay in bed for the rest of the day."

Andy rolled her eyes. "Like that'll happen," she said, then asked sarcastically, "Did he use superglue?"

"Actually, he used something better," Alex called after her. Andy turned around and waited, curious.

"Stevi and Mike are standing guard over Dad so that he won't be tempted to get up. Mike is prepared to use brute force if he has to," she added with a wide grin.

Andy smiled, then realized what that

meant. "Mike's not at work?" she asked in surprise.

To remain in San Diego, the former undercover DEA agent had resigned his post and joined the local police department. And as the new detective on the force, he was putting in a lot of long hours to prove he could be an asset to the department.

"Stevi called him and told Mike what happened to Dad and he immediately told his captain that he was taking some personal time and left early."

"Bet that didn't go over well," Andy guessed.

"The captain's a friend of Dad's," Alex reminded her.

Their father was everyone's friend. "Well, that should make Dad feel a little better," she speculated.

"It's not like it's a surprise," Alex said. "Dad knows how important he is to all of us."

With the matter of her father temporarily taken care of and wheels set in motion to prevent the sale of the inn, Andy crossed back to her sister.

"You look awfully pale—even more than usual."

"Always the flatterer," Alex quipped, dismissing her.

Andy would have dropped the subject if it wasn't for the fact that she saw Alex pressing her hand against her belly as if that would somehow simultaneously harness the pain and keep the baby in place.

"When are you due again?" Andy asked. "I get you and Cris mixed up."

"I'm the pretty one," Alex explained.

"If that's short for pretty annoying, you'll get no argument here," Andy told her. "Now, when are you due?"

Not soon enough, Alex thought.

"The end of December, beginning of January, sometime in there," she said out loud.

She was having trouble catching her breath. Her little tenant was definitely pressing against organs that should have been off-limits. She really felt as if she'd been pregnant forever.

"Does that kid have a calendar in there?" Andy deadpanned.

"I think the baby's a minimalist," Alex told her. "Wouldn't accept a calendar even though I tried to convince her that she needed one."

Andy looked at her in surprise. "Wait a minute, you just called the baby 'she.' I thought you said you didn't want the doctor to tell you if the baby was going to be a girl or a boy."

"I didn't," Alex agreed. Then, before Andy could ask anything further, Alex told her, "I'm just using positive reinforcement."

"Then you do want a girl?" Andy asked. This was getting confusing.

"Of course I do," Alex said with feeling. "Girls are all I know how to deal with."

Well, that didn't hold any water, in Andy's opinion. "News flash, Alex. Your nephew's a boy and you manage just fine with him. Bigger news flash," she went on, "you don't do all that well with females if you're basing it on getting along with Cris, Stevi and me."

"Well, aren't you just a little ray of sunshine," Alex snapped.

"Just calling it like I see it, Alex," Andy

said brightly. "Now, do you want me to take you to the doctor or the ER?"

"What I want is for you to go away," Alex told her. "I'll be fine—I'll be even better if you stop hovering over me."

Shifting gears, Alex addressed a couple who'd just walked in. Rain was dripping off the umbrella they had huddled under as they entered. "Hello, welcome to Ladera by the Sea. How can I be of service?"

Andy knew that further discussion was tabled for now. She stepped to the side, allowing the soggy couple to approach the desk.

"I'll check on you later," she told Alex, smiling at the newcomers.

"Just check on Dad, see if he needs anything," Alex said before she turned her attention back to the inn's newest guests.

"Is it always like this?" the woman asked as she brushed rain from her hair and coat.

Alex gave the couple her best smile. "Actually, we've been in a drought for several years now. This rain is a welcome change."

The woman's husband frowned. "Well,

I wish it had waited until we were on our way home."

"There's a cozy fire going in the common room. And we'll do our best to make you forget about the rain, sir," Alex promised.

Good luck with that, Andy thought as she made her way to her dad's room.

Her father had chosen to occupy a bedroom in the newer wing on the first floor rather than his original bedroom, which was in the old part of the inn. He'd shared that bedroom with their mother and after she'd died, as much as he cherished her memory, he just couldn't bring himself to sleep in that bedroom without her.

As she wound her way through the newer wing, Andy could hear the wind picking up. The howling almost sounded mournful.

She really hoped this wouldn't affect business adversely. As a rule, late November to the end of March was officially referred to as Southern California's rainy season. However, over the past decade nature had more or less taken a holiday and hadn't lived up to its reputation, especially in the past six years.

So much so that she'd forgotten just how fierce a winter storm here could be. It didn't just rain in California, she mused, remembering a piece of a lyric from an old song, it poured.

Well, they could certainly use the rain, she mused as she turned down another hallway. Hopefully the rain wouldn't turn into a flood.

Arriving at her father's door, Andy knocked once, then tried the doorknob. When she felt it give, she let herself in.

Not only were Stevi and Mike there, just as Alex had said, but so was Cris and her son, Ricky. Ricky was in the midst of giving his grandfather a blow-by-blow description of his day at school. Ricky could be trusted to go on talking until he ran out of words.

The boy seemed to be getting taller by the month. At this rate, he would be towering over all of them before he reached his teens. With lively eyes and honey-brown hair that was just a wee bit unruly, he had all the makings of a heart-throb when he got to be a little older.

Cris, Andy thought, was really going to have her hands full.

Andy made eye contact with her father. "Room for one more?" she asked, slipping inside. She had to burrow her way in between Cris and Stevi.

"One more what, Aunt Andy?" Ricky asked, temporarily halting his long, involved narrative.

"One more person," Cris told her son. "You can take my place," she volunteered. "I've got to go back to the kitchen and get dinner started."

"You're working too hard, Cris," her father chided. "Have Jorge do more of the cooking."

"Said the man who practically worked himself to death," Andy interjected.

Richard waved his hand dismissively, indicating that he wasn't about to have that discussion. "Where have you been?" he asked her.

Before she could decide whether or not she was going to be honest or fabricate something for the time being, Stevi jumped in with, "Does he still have all his teeth?"

"Who?" Richard asked, bewildered as he looked from one daughter to the other. "Who are you talking about?"

"The lawyer Andy went to corner," Stevi told her father matter-of-factly.

Richard's head snapped back to his youngest. "Andy, you didn't," he said, a stern note in his voice. Sternness was as close as he ever came to registering disapproval.

Stevi laughed dryly. "Dad, this is Andy and she's a Roman. Of course she did."

CHAPTER NINE

RICHARD DUG HIS fists into the mattress on either side of him, struggling to push himself up to a sitting position. "I don't want you girls to worry about this. I'll handle it."

Mike, standing on one side of the headboard, placed his hand on the older man's shoulder and very gently pushed him down again. When Richard looked at him, Mike merely smiled.

The tables had turned. A year ago it was Richard who had been pushing him back down in bed because he'd been shot. Mike knew how hard it was to remain in bed when you were accustomed to being in charge, but that didn't change anything.

It was clear that no one in the room was about to allow him to get up out of bed.

"Dad, you're the one who always emphasized that family supports one another,"

Andy reminded him. "We're a family and we'll deal with this together. But we can't focus on that if we're worried about you. Now your job, your *only* job," she said as she took one of his hands in both of hers, "is to get better. Do I make myself clear, young man?"

Richard smiled weakly at her. "I think you've got our roles reversed, Andy."

"Oh, I think I've got a clear picture of them." Releasing his hand, she stepped back, away from her father's bed. "Now, you rest and let us handle everything." Her eyes shifted toward Stevi and Mike. "See that he stays in bed until at least tomorrow morning. Sit on him if you have to."

The latter instruction was directed at Mike.

The detective grinned. "You know, if you're still trying to decide on a career, Andy, I'd suggest drill sergeant."

"I'll think about it," she replied as she left the room.

"DID YOU GET a chance to call Wyatt yet?" Andy asked the minute she returned to the reception desk.

Alex nodded. "I called him at his office in LA but that lawyer he brought in to help Cris is away on business. He won't be back until next Monday, at the earliest."

That was not what she wanted to hear. Andy pressed her lips together in frustration. "Well, we'll just have to tell MacArthur we need more time."

"Think he'll give it to us?"

"Honestly? I don't know," Andy admitted. "But since this is the first we're hearing about this, I really can't see them giving all of us the bum's rush and throwing us—*and* a venerable elementary school teacher—out of our home."

"That's right, Ms. Carlyle would be out of a home, too," Alex realized. "I forgot about that." She smiled at Andy ruefully. "What's wrong with me? That's not something that would just slip my mind."

"It's okay, Alex. You're pregnant. Your brain cells are focused on that little human being you're busy forming."

"That's no excuse," Alex complained.

"Works for me," Andy told her. "Now, stop beating yourself up and start thinking about what we can do to stop the county or state or whatever from grabbing our land."

"Whatever we do, it's going to have to involve publicity. We need the public on our side."

"Brave little inn versus big, bad government," Andy said, creating the headline. "Might work. Wyatt knows famous people, doesn't he?" Her brother-in-law was a writer, something she'd toyed with becoming herself. For the most part, Wyatt wrote screenplays, which allowed him to rub elbows with big-name actors, directors and producers.

"He does. What are you thinking?"

"Well, among other things, we could organize a fund-raiser, invite some of the people Wyatt's dealt with. People are drawn to celebrities. If they knew they'd be mingling with names, they'll be more likely to attend. And donate. We're going to need money for a good lawyer."

Alex stared at her. Andy became aware of it after a few beats had gone by where she was doing all the talking. "What?" she asked, stopping abruptly.

"This is a side of you I've never seen before. You're good at this, aren't you?"

Andy shrugged. "Desperate times require desperate measures," she said. Shifting gears, she came up with another idea. "A fund-raiser's going to take some time to organize. But we can do something else immediately."

"Such as?" Alex asked.

"A letter-writing campaign—especially if I write the blueprint for the letter and everyone can download it, signing their name to it as is, if they want. Or they can use it as an example and create their own letter. I don't care which as long as letters get sent and he gets inundated."

"He?" Alex asked, trying to follow Andy's train of thought.

"The illustrious Logan MacArthur," Andy said, uttering the name as if it tasted terrible on her tongue. "Anyway, that's the plan for now."

Was it her imagination, or was her sister looking even more pregnant now than she had a few hours ago? This baby was going to be huge, she thought, pitying Alex.

"In the meantime, why don't you take a break, go have some dinner?" she suggested. Glancing at her watch, she suddenly became aware of the time. "Shouldn't Wyatt be here by now?" she asked.

"When I called him he said that the rain is making it very difficult to travel. He already assumed that he was going to be late." Alex laughed softly to herself. "You know what happens around here when it rains—some people drive in slow motion, others race like crazy—as if they were going to get ahead of the rain. Accidents waiting to happen."

Everything that Alex said was true, but there was no point in any further discussion. Andy had things she needed to do— as did her sister. The first of which was to have a healthy dinner.

"Alex, dinner, now," Andy ordered. "You know how grumpy you get when you haven't eaten."

"Almost as grumpy as when I'm being ordered around by my kid sister," Alex responded. "But since you offered to take over and I *am* hungry, I'll take that dinner break. It should be quiet. I don't have any reservations on the books until tomorrow morning."

"We might get walk-ins," Andy pointed out.

"You mean swim-ins, don't you? Think it's going to let up tonight?" Alex asked, moving over to the large bay window that looked out on the front walk and the ocean in the distance.

It had been coming down pretty heavily. "If it doesn't, someone should start building a boat and collecting two of everything," Andy muttered. "But it can't keep up like this for long."

"I'll hold you to that," Alex said, and for a moment Andy couldn't help thinking about the obstacle the rain could present if Alex had to get to the hospital quickly.

"I knew you would," Andy murmured, and started mentally drafting the letter she was going to post on the inn's Facebook page.

APPARENTLY, ANDY THOUGHT the next day, remembering her comment to Alex about the

wet weather not going on forever, Mother
Nature had other ideas. Although the rain
had abated a couple of times during the
course of the past twenty-four hours, it always came back with a vengeance. It made
her wonder uneasily if this was somehow
an omen of things to come.

The rain was threatening to depress her,
bringing darker thoughts to the foreground.
That wasn't something she was accustomed
to and she wanted to head this funk off before it took hold.

It wasn't easy, but she forced herself to
focus on the letter-writing campaign.

She and her sisters had gotten on their
cell phones, calling everyone they knew.
Everyone their father knew. The crux of the
matter was to spread the word that the inn
was in jeopardy and that its doors might
be permanently closed because the state
wanted the land the inn was built on.

Andy was banking on outrage saving
the day.

"And please," Andy said to the umpteenth person she had called, "if you can
get your friends to send letters, too, we'd

appreciate it. If you don't know what to write, go to Ladera's Facebook page and just copy the letter I've posted there. And be sure to mail it to Logan MacArthur." She rattled off the address of his firm. That, too, was posted on the website. "Time is really important so please write and mail that letter as soon as you hang up."

Terminating the call a couple of minutes later, Andy leaned back in her chair and closed her eyes. She'd been at this for several hours, trying to reach as many people as she could—friends, friends of friends and past guests at the inn. Everyone she'd spoken to had promised to help.

Momentarily satisfied, Andy smiled to herself. She was determined to flood Mac-Arthur's office with letters. She wanted the man to realize that he was being instrumental in helping to close down an icon, a well-loved inn that had seen more than its share of special events, and was at the center of so many countless happy memories.

If possible, she was twice as committed to saving the inn today as she was before because last night it had suddenly occurred to her that if it was destroyed, there was nothing to stop the same thing happening to the family cemetery.

She absolutely refused to contemplate that. Her mother and Uncle Dan were both buried there, not to mention several other family members from years gone by.

The thought of that being destroyed for development was too much to bear. Even if they received enough notice to remove and transfer the coffins, it went against everything she believed in to disturb something that was supposed to have been an eternal resting place.

This had to work, she told herself. It just had to.

Taking a deep breath, Andy picked up the phone again and began to dial.

"IS IT TRUE?"

Startled, Andy turned toward the source of the voice asking her the question. The rain had let up for a little while, although the dark clouds all remained in attendance and the weather forecast was for more rain before nightfall. But since the rain had temporarily halted, Andy had taken the opportunity to go out on the back veranda to get a little air.

Ms. Carlyle was standing just inside the threshold, waiting for an answer.

Andy had a feeling she knew what their only in-house permanent resident was referring to, but just in case she was wrong, she feigned ignorance.

"Is what true?" she asked.

Impatience creased Ms Carlyle's wrinkled brow. "The rumors about the inn, of course. That it's closing its doors."

"Not if any of us can help it," Andy told her fiercely.

Impatience was replaced with a sadness that Andy had never seen on the woman's face before. "So it *is* true," Ms. Carlyle concluded.

Andy was determined not to dwell on the possibility of losing the fight. "Let's just say that someone is trying to force us out, but this inn has been in Dad's family for over a hundred and twenty years and there have been a lot of rough times. This is just another rough patch, that's all. But we are all staying put."

Moving closer to her, Ms. Carlyle studied her very closely, the woman's sharp gray eyes defying her to lie. "Are you worried, Andrea?"

Denial was Andy's first response. Ms. Carlyle's gaze never wavered. Pinned down, Andy finally shrugged and admitted, "Maybe. I wouldn't be human if I wasn't a little worried."

Ms. Carlyle nodded slowly. Then she said something that surprised Andy. "Is there anything I can do to help?"

"If you have any favors you can call in, now would be the time," Andy said, only half kidding. "Other than that, you can sign and mail in the letter I have posted on the inn's Facebook page if you don't feel up to writing your own. I could print the letter up for you."

"You think I don't know what Facebook is?" Ms. Carlyle snapped. "I might be old, Andrea, but I'm not dead. I keep up with what's going on around me. But you may print it up for me if you like," she said magnanimously. "Sending your letter rather than my own will save time."

Beaming, Andy was off in search of the nearest laptop. "Right away," she called back. "Don't go anywhere!"

"THINK THIS WILL make a difference?" Cris asked the following day as Andy dragged out yet another duffel bag full of letters to take to the post office.

Since the campaign got under way, there had been four duffel bags worth of letters mailed out. This made five and with luck, there would be plenty more.

The biggest surprise was that people were writing old-fashioned snail-mail letters—and somehow they'd taken it upon themselves to send those letters care of the inn to show their support rather than directly to MacArthur as she'd instructed.

She was more than happy to be the middleman in this.

The campaign was going full tilt by email, too. That should be filling up the lawyer's in-box, she thought in smug satisfaction.

"Well, it certainly can't hurt," Andy told Cris. "Maybe if those bloodsuckers at the law firm see how important the inn is to everyone, they'll suggest that the government find another piece of land to build on. A piece of land that wouldn't require them to shatter several lifetimes' worth of work."

"Did that lawyer ever tell Dad what the government planned to build here?" Cris asked.

Shivering, she pulled the shawl about her shoulders tighter. The temperature had dropped several degrees, ushering in a chill. Looking up at the sky, she felt that the rain wasn't far off. Again.

"Dad was vague, saying something about it possibly being a theater for the performing arts. Nothing positive, but I don't understand why they'd even need land by the ocean that's outside of town for that kind of event site."

She shook her head.

"But I didn't want to ply Dad with questions and get him worked up. I figure that whatever their plan is, it definitely won't be worth demolishing the inn for. The inn is well loved by the community and they won't welcome anything that goes up in its place."

She glanced down at the duffel bag, which had yet to be hefted into the trunk.

"These letters will testify to that," she gloated.

Cris remained quiet for a moment as Andy popped the truck. "What if this doesn't work?" she asked.

Andy looked up sharply. It wasn't a question she had failed to ask herself. But it wasn't something she wanted to dwell on.

"Then we'll try something else until we find something that does," Andy replied. "Wyatt's lawyer has to come back from his business sometime."

"And if that doesn't work?" Cris persisted.

Andy could tell that Cris didn't believe they could make a difference. That to pull this off, Andy would have to be a miracle worker. They'd all have to be.

But she read the truth in her sister's expression: none of them were.

"Then we'll try something else, until

we find something that does work. Cris, my answer's not going to change no matter how many times you ask. Somewhere, somehow, we're going to find the one thing that'll stop those idiots in Sacramento from taking a wrecking ball to the inn."

"This would be a good time for one of us to know a state senator or a congressman," Cris said wistfully.

"Maybe we can kidnap one," Andy deadpanned.

She'd sounded too serious, she realized the next minute from the wary look on Cris's face.

"Kidding," Andy reassured her older sister. "Just kidding."

Bracing herself, Andy got ready to lift the duffel bag and place it in the trunk. Not only that, but she was going to need to secure it. Her first run had taught her that, when the mail had gone flying out of the unsecured bag, covering the entire trunk with letters.

As she wrapped her arms around the bag, she found herself being gently elbowed out of the way by Shane, who lifted the bag as if it was empty.

"Thanks," Andy said. "But aren't you supposed to be out building something?" she asked Cris's husband.

Tall and dark-haired, the ruggedly handsome contractor grinned. "In case you haven't noticed, it's been raining," he said. "It's a little hard to work in the rain. For one thing, the smell of wet wood is awful. We're waiting for it to let up for more than a few minutes at a time. I can take this to the post office for you."

Before she could protest, he added, "I need to do something before I go stir-crazy, so you'd be doing me a big favor. By the way, my crew all signed letters and mailed them out for you."

"Thanks, I appreciate it. And if you want to do this mail run for me, go right ahead." She could use the time to make more phone calls, although she was coming close to the end of her list.

Shane leaned in for a second, long enough to make his own request. "Do me a favor. Keep an eye on Cris. I think the baby might come early."

Clearly, Shane was dealing with a case of first baby jitters. It might be old hat for Cris, but it was Shane's first. First-time dads were usually nervous wrecks as the due date grew closer—or so she'd heard.

Out loud Andy said, "Sure, no problem."

"What's no problem?" Cris asked as she and Andy went back inside.

"Keeping my eye on you to make sure you don't deliver without Shane. That's kind of like enforcing poetic justice," she commented.

Cris looked at her, confused. "How do you figure that?"

"Well, Shane was there when that baby was created, so he should be there when the baby arrives, don't you think?"

Cris laughed, shaking her head. She kept her shawl wrapped around her for the time being, waiting to warm up. "You know, for a would-be writer, you have a horrible way of putting things."

"Because of your condition, I'll ignore

that. So how are you feeling?" Andy asked as they walked.

"Like I weigh five hundred pounds and have always been pregnant," Cris replied, sighing.

"Well, you *haven't* always been this way," Andy assured her. "And I've got the pictures to prove it. Don't worry, Cris," she patted her sister's arm. "It'll be over very soon."

Cris gave her a weary look. "Said the woman who's never been pregnant."

"I might never have been pregnant, but I know how long a full-term pregnancy lasts," Andy said in her own defense.

"Education and experience are two completely different things," Cris pointed out. "I'm down to counting minutes."

Any further debate on the subject was tabled when the sisters saw who had just stepped into the inn, followed by sheets of rain.

Logan MacArthur, his topcoat drenched, was dragging an equally drenched duffel bag behind him. Stopping before the reception desk, he hefted the duffel bag and deposited it on top. A small puddle formed beneath it.

"Just what is all this?" Logan demanded, staring straight at Andy.

"Well," she said, stretching out the word as she opened the bag—for the most part, the rain hadn't managed to get inside. "It appears to be mail," she declared, then looked right at Logan and gave him a huge grin. "I'll take a wild stab at it and say mail."

"I *know* it's mail," he answered through gritted teeth, "but why is it addressed to me?"

"How else can it reach you?" Andy asked innocently.

It was clear that Logan was struggling with his temper. "*Why* is it reaching me?"

"Well, this is another wild guess," Andy said, "But maybe it's so that you can see just how much the inn means to everyone around here."

"And I assume that you're the one behind this letter-writing campaign?"

"I was the one who mentioned that the inn was going to be destroyed and we were going to be thrown out of our home if you didn't have a change of heart," Andy replied, leaving it at that.

"My heart has nothing to do with this," he informed her.

"Nobody can do anything without a heart," she retorted stubbornly. "Not even you, so there has to be a heart in there somewhere, no matter how small."

Just for a second, she had rendered the lawyer speechless.

CHAPTER TEN

GATHERING HIMSELF TOGETHER—and curbing the impulse to tell this young woman what he thought of her—Logan said evenly, "What I think, what I feel about the matter, has no bearing on my responsibility to see this through for the firm's client."

Andy looked at him as if he was deserving of pity. She was not about to let it slide.

"Why would you take a case you don't feel passionate about?"

He had never met anyone like this woman. Anyone so naive and idealistic. But she was young—probably had never been out in the workforce. Probably still in college. Did her father even know what she was up to? he had to wonder.

He operated on an even keel, able to see any goal through efficiently, not allowing his emotions to get in the way because he had no emotions regarding the cases he represented.

But this woman seemed to be able to set him off within seconds, igniting reactions he'd never felt before, forcing him to actually keep a tight rein on his temper. A temper he'd never known he had before coming in contact with Andrea Roman.

"Because, Ms. Roman, it's my job and if I do it well and the senior partners are satisfied, it will continue being my job. I didn't take the case—the firm I work for did. Passion has nothing to do with deciding what I do and don't get to work on."

And that, he sincerely hoped, was that.

He should have known better.

"In other words," she said, her voice a mixture of anger and pity, "you're doing it for the money."

"Most people work for the money, yes." And he doubted that she was as altruistic as she was trying to portray.

For just a moment, anger gave way to pity again as she told him, "Only the ones who wind up burned out way before their time."

This so-called debate showed all the earmarks of going on forever, with neither of them convincing the other.

"Well, I'd love to stand here and debate this with you, but I have to get back before the roads become impassable." He turned up the collar of his overcoat. "If I were you, Ms. Roman, I'd stop beating the bushes for letter writers and start looking for a place to relocate."

"MacArthur," Andy called after the lawyer as he began to walk away.

Still struggling to maintain his cool, Logan paused and turned his head. "What?"

Andy rounded the desk and hefted the duffel bag off the counter, then unceremoniously pushed it into his arms. "You forgot your mail."

He let the bag drop to the floor before him. "I didn't forget it, I'm leaving it here."

"Can't do that," she informed him brightly. "It's addressed to you care of the inn, not anyone here. Can't be tampering with the United States mail, now, can we?"

Her expression was that of total innocence, but she was laughing at him. He could see it in her eyes. He felt his body temperature go up half a dozen degrees.

Logan glared at her a moment before he took hold of the duffel bag again and threw it over his shoulder, fireman style.

Breaking his own rules, he said, "You have an annoying personality, you know that?"

Andy smiled beatifically. "Right back at you."

Biting his tongue, Logan marched across the floor to the entrance.

She stood and watched him walk out into the rain. It was still coming down in sheets. He was going to be drenched by the time he reached his car. Of course, he was already drenched, so what did it matter?

"I hope he drowns," she declared to no one in particular.

Cris was the only one within earshot. "Andy…"

She turned to face her sister. "You can 'Andy' me all you want. That doesn't change the way that I feel about that man." Glancing back toward the door to reassure herself that he had actually left, she turned back to Cris. "He can't win. We just can't let him win," she repeated with feeling.

Cris cocked her head, studying her. "Are you saying that because you don't want to lose the old homestead, or because you just don't want to lose to him?"

"It used to be the first," Andy admitted. "But now it's both." The corners of her mouth curved up. "Nothing wrong with multiple goals, Cris," she said before she got back to work.

"Isn't it ever going to stop?" Andy lamented, giving in to a moment of dejection. It had been raining off and on—mainly on—for over a week now. She had almost lost track of the days, they were all so very gray. There had been several power outages reported all over the county as one storm came in on the heels of another. So far, the electric outages had missed the inn, but she had a feeling it was just a matter of time before it was their turn.

As if things weren't gloomy enough.

"Eventually it has to," Stevi answered.

She was on the reception desk today because Alex had woken up feeling more out of it than usual. "A month ago, everyone was complaining about the drought," she reminded Andy.

"That's becoming a fond memory at this point."

"I want to get married, Andy," Stevi said out of the blue.

Andy turned away from the bay window and crossed back to the desk. "I kind of got that impression from the engagement ring you're wearing."

But Stevi shook her head sadly. "I want to get married here, at the inn. Before there is no inn."

The fact that Stevi was feeling this way surprised Andy. "Don't go writing it off yet. If nothing else, we can get injunctions, fight this thing in the courts, drag it out as long as possible. We just need Wyatt's lawyer behind us. We'll buy ourselves more time, emphasize the little David versus big Goliath angle, drum up more goodwill. And, in the end," Andy concluded, "we'll win."

Stevi looked into her eyes. "You really believe that?"

"Yes," Andy responded without any hesitation.

"Why?" Stevi pressed. She'd never needed reassurance before about anything, but she needed it now. It felt as if the very ground was opening up beneath her feet. The most constant thing in her life, other than her family, was the inn.

"Because I have to," Andy answered. "It's as simple as that. There's a solution to this problem—we just haven't found it yet, but that doesn't mean it's not out there." She stopped to squeeze her sister's hand. "Have a little faith."

Stevi took in a long, cleansing breath and then let it out. "Okay, I will," she allowed. "But I still want to get married here. How about this weekend?"

That stunned Andy. "That's four days away! That's not enough time to organize a wedding. You of all people know that."

Stevi had organized Alex and Cris's double wedding last Christmas. She had been a veritable bridezilla—despite only being the wedding planner—through a good part of it, until it appeared to all be on track.

But this was different. No pageantry required.

"Mike and I already have the license. We took that out at the beginning of the month," she explained. "And we don't want anything fancy, just the family and maybe a few friends."

Andy didn't want Stevi to look back on her wedding in the years to come and feel as if she was cheated because some lawyer was threatening to take away their home.

"What about a wedding dress?" Andy demanded.

Stevi had that covered, too. "I've already tried on Mom's. It fits."

"How about a tux for Shane?"

Stevi shrugged. Mike was a no-frills guy. "He doesn't need a tux. A suit will be just as good."

Andy paused for a moment. "Mike's about Wyatt's size, isn't he?"

Stevi thought for a moment, trying to remember seeing the two men standing side by side. "I guess."

Andy was fairly sure they were not only approximately the same height, but the same build, as well. "I think the tux Wyatt wore to his wedding is boxed in the attic. We can bring it down and have Mike try it on. I'm pretty sure it'll fit.

"Cris can make the wedding cake and we'll have Jorge take care of the dinner so we don't tire Cris out."

And then Andy grinned just before declaring, in a pseudo-English accent, "By George, I think we've just fashioned ourselves one express wedding."

Stevi threw her arms around Andy and hugged her really hard. "You're a crazy person, you know that, right? Lucky for you I like crazy people."

"Lucky for you I don't take offense," Andy countered with a laugh, returning her hug.

One problem down, a thousand to go, Andy couldn't help thinking.

FOR THE NEXT three days, the save-the-inn campaign took a backseat to arranging Stevi and Mike's wedding. Because she was the only Roman sister of the remaining three who wasn't pregnant, Andy handled most of the decorating in the common room where the wedding was going to be.

Stevi would have preferred the kind of outdoor wedding Alex and Cris had had, but the weather was still refusing to cooperate. The rain had stopped for now, but the forecast was riding the fence between predictions of rain and predictions of partly sunny.

She was an optimist, but Andy knew better than to bet on a sunny day.

"Better safe than sorry," Andy murmured for the hundredth time, wishing she could give Stevi the kind of wedding she wanted. In fact, Stevi was dealing with the venue better than she was.

Andy frowned as she climbed the ladder to the second step from the top, stretching to reach the spot where she wanted to hang the banner that proclaimed: Happy Forever, Stevi & Mike!

"You know, only geniuses and fools talk to themselves. Which one are you?"

Startled, Andy dropped the edge of the

banner. One hand wrapped around a rung of the ladder, she turned slightly only to find herself looking down at the man she regarded as the bane of her existence.

"Genius," she answered without hesitation. "And if you're thinking of tipping this ladder over, don't. If I fall, hit my head and slip into a coma, everyone will still know that you were the one who did it."

He watched as she carefully made her way down. "Is that what you think of me? As someone who'd deliberately cause an accident?"

Andy retrieved the banner, and holding it with one hand she began to climb back up the ladder.

"Hard to have warm and toasty thoughts about the man who's pulling the very foundation of your life out from under you." Andy froze when she saw Logan take hold of one side of the ladder. "What do you think you're doing?" she asked sharply.

"Relax, I'm holding the ladder steady so you *don't* fall." His mouth curved slightly. "No offense, but I don't think I would put it past you not to stage something."

"I'm not that devious," she informed him.

Wavering, she decided she'd take Logan at his word and stretched as far as she could to attach the corner of the banner to the hook that had been mounted earlier.

"Oh, yes, you are," he said with complete conviction.

Satisfied the banner would hold, she came back down the ladder to face him.

"Let's cut to the chase," she said. "Why are you here?"

He had thought of nothing else but the case since he'd left here the other day, hefting a soggy duffel bag filled with letters. More kept coming every day. He still intended to do right by his clients, but there had to be something about the inn for so many people to come to its defense. Perhaps raising the selling price would help ease the pain.

"I've come to make your father a better offer," he told her.

She looked at him for a long moment.

"Unless it involves you and your clients fading into the night and never darkening our doorstep again, it's not a better offer and we're not interested."

Everyone was interested in more money. It was the one lesson his parents had taught him. People came with price tags, with bottom lines. The trick was to find it.

"I've persuaded them to offer you and your family more money," he repeated. "And I'd like to speak to your father."

Facing him squarely, she fisted her hands on her hips. "Let's get this clear once and for all, MacArthur. There isn't enough money in the world to get my family to give up our rights to the inn."

It occurred to him that she was cute when she had steam coming out of her ears. The next moment, he forced himself to tamp down his reaction and focus on what was really important: getting her to come around and be reasonable.

"I don't believe that."

Her breath came out in an angry, weary huff. "That, MacArthur, is your problem, not mine. Now, if you don't mind, I have a wedding to prepare for."

That pulled him up short. "Yours?" he asked.

"Hardly. My sister Stephanie and her fiancé, Mike—a detective on the Ladera Police Department I might add—are getting married. Ordinarily, they would be getting married after the holidays, but you've spooked her so much, she's afraid if she waits, she won't be able to get married here."

They stared at each other.

"All the Roman women have gotten married here since the inn was first opened," she told him, her eyes narrowing to small laser beams.

"Why hardly?" he asked.

She blinked. "What?"

"When I asked if the wedding you were getting ready for was yours, you said 'hardly.' I was just asking why you responded that way."

Like it or not, she kept stirring his curiosity, making it impossible for him to remain distant, impartial and uninvolved. But he was fighting that reaction as hard as he could.

She had already starting climbing the
ladder again, but his question brought
Andy back down, a bantam rooster ready
to take on a big game cock for control of
the yard.

"So now you're trying to psychoana-
lyze me?" she asked incredulously. "The
answer, MacArthur, is very simple. I said
'hardly' because Stevi has a fiancé and I
do not."

"Maybe if you stopped biting people's
heads off when they talk to you," he theo-
rized, "that situation might change."

"Save your romantic advice for your
wife, MacArthur," she informed him
coolly. "I can live without it."

"I don't have a wife." The response had
been automatic and he berated himself for
it. She had just caused him to break another
one of his rules: his private life was to remain just that. Private.

"What a surprise."

He should leave. The woman was impossible and there was no getting through to
her, no reasoning with her. He didn't even
know why he was bothering to try. After

all, it was her father whose name was on the deed, and by all rights, Richard Roman was the one who was in the position to accept or reject the offer.

But he had a feeling that if he did approach the family patriarch in the man's present weakened condition, the firebrand he was talking to would have his head.

"Answer a question for me," he requested.

"I'm not making any promises," she told him in an uninterested voice. "Go ahead."

"Why are you people so stubborn?" he wanted to know. The offer from the state was not insignificant. It certainly would allow them to buy another inn somewhere else. "It's just a building. Wood, nails, a few coats of paint. You could take the money, go somewhere and build a better inn. A more modern one," he suggested.

He watched her eyes as his words sank in.

She wasn't buying it.

"We don't want a better inn, we want this inn. It's our heritage, our history. You can't put a price on that."

"That's where you're wrong. You can put a price on anything."

She stopped and looked at him. Really looked at him.

"You mean that, don't you?" Andy asked him in a whisper. There was no antagonism in her voice, no anger. Just wonder and...sadness.

"Yes," he replied without a moment's hesitation.

What she said next caught Logan completely off guard.

"I am so sorry."

"Sorry about what?" he asked, confused. Why would she say that?

"Sorry that you never had anything in your life that you cared about, that meant the world to you. Sorry that you never had anything you wanted to protect."

She regarded him for another long moment.

"Your parents sent you to boarding school when you were very young, didn't they?"

He almost accused her of making a lucky

guess but managed to stop himself. "That's none of your business."

"Actually, in a way it is. If that affected the way you regard things, the way you could—or couldn't—relate to things, then your being sent to boarding school most certainly is my business."

She annoyed and impressed him at the same time, effectively tying his insides—not to mention his very ability to think clearly—in knots.

"You studying to be a lawyer?" he asked out of the blue.

"Heaven forbid," was Andy's immediate—and honest—response. "Why?"

"Because, you could probably argue the ears off a brass monkey. If not off, then at least seriously damage them," he added.

He couldn't help wondering what she would have been like in the courtroom. The woman just didn't know how to back off once she fixated on a target.

"Is that what lawyers do? Argue with brass monkeys?" Andy asked, doing little to hide her amusement at his choice of words.

If he continued to remain here, exchanging words with this woman, he did not want to be held accountable for his actions. It was time for him to take his leave.

"I'd better go before the roads are rendered completely impassible," he told her and then, just like that, he walked out of the room and, she assumed, out of the inn.

Maybe next time the road will be declared impassible before you get here, Andy thought, getting back to work. One could only hope.

CHAPTER ELEVEN

LOOKING BACK, ANDY would have been willing to bet money that she had seen the last
of Mr. Logan MacArthur, at least until the
sun became more than just a myth and
dried up the residual flooding. Until after
Stevi's wedding, anyway—especially since
it was tomorrow.

She would have been wrong.

Approximately forty-five minutes after
he made his exit, a far from happy Logan
MacArthur returned to the inn.

Andy had just finished decorating the
common room for the next day's festivi-
ties and was about to call Silvio to tell him
that he could have his ladder back when
she plowed into Logan as she was leaving
the room.

She could feel her heart thud against her
rib cage.

"You're back," she said in disbelief as she automatically covered her heart with her hand. The next moment, Andy regrouped. "If you've come back to get a second crack at tipping me over, I'm afraid you're too late. I've finished putting up the decorations and I'm too busy to listen to whatever new angle you've come up with to make stealing the inn look like less than a crime. My sister's getting married tomorrow and I've still got a lot of things left to do so forgive me for being rude but go away!" she ordered, shouting the two words at him.

"Believe me, I'd like nothing better," Logan told her, frustration etching itself into his features.

"So what's stopping you?" It wasn't as if she, or anyone else at the inn, was trying to detain him. Quite the opposite.

"Those roads I've told you about? The ones I need in order to leave? Well, they've washed out."

This was the first she'd heard about that. She'd been too busy working to listen to the news. She hoped this wouldn't stop some of the wedding guests from coming.

She knew that wouldn't have stopped her if she wanted to get away from someone. "Find different roads," she told Logan in a no-nonsense voice.

"There aren't any," he said evenly, carefully enunciating each word. "The freeway is inaccessible. It seems that right now Ladera, for all intents and purposes, has become an island. Nobody can come in, nobody can go out," he explained, using hand gestures to further illustrate his point.

Andy's eyes never left his face. "I don't believe you."

It was on the tip of his tongue to ask her what she thought he had to gain by lying, but Logan was certain that her answer would only make him angry. Or angrier, because he was already angry.

He let it slide.

"I'd tell you to go see for yourself, but the weather bureau is issuing flash flood warnings for the area, and if you try driving toward the freeway you just might wind up floating out to sea." He'd had a hard time turning the vehicle around, fighting the rain for control of his car. Navigation had been nothing short of a challenge.

"And you came back here because?" Andy drew out the last word.

As she continued watching him, she could see that the man was struggling with what he had to say. The expression on his face was one close to pain as he grudgingly admitted, "Because I need a room for the night."

Wow, talk about an ironic turn. She looked at him for another long moment.

Her mouth smiled practically on its own accord. "I believe this is the part where I say there's no room at the inn."

Before Logan could comment, they heard, "Andy, we have room."

Both Logan and she turned to see that her father had come in.

"I know that, Dad," she said, without so much as a blink of an eye. "But if MacArthur and his people have their way, there won't be any rooms available very soon. But more important, what are you doing up and wandering around?" she asked, crossing to him. "You're still supposed to be taking it easy, remember? Tomorrow's a big day and you want to be up for it."

"I wanted to see how the decorating was coming along. And besides, I need to be able to maneuver Stevi down the aisle tomorrow," he told Andy softly, but in no uncertain terms. Changing subjects, he told his daughter to ask Dorothy to get the Windsor Room ready for Mr. MacArthur.

Logan looked at the older man, surprised and grateful. "I appreciate that, Mr. Roman. Especially under the circumstances."

"We've never turned anyone away as long as we had a room for them," he told the younger man.

"Do you want me to sign in at reception, sir?" Logan asked. "I'll pay for the room in full ahead of time."

Richard waved away the last sentence. "That won't be necessary."

As if to punctuate his statement, the rain lashed against the bay window, rattling it like a petitioner, trying to get in.

The wind howled louder.

"It's not like you can go anywhere,"

Andy grudgingly pointed out, not looking at either of them.

Richard redirected his attention to something closer to his heart. "You've done a nice job, Andy," he said, gazing around. "Stevi will be very pleased."

His youngest smiled, and Richard changed topics again. "Why don't you bring our guest to reception and then to the dining area? You probably haven't had a chance to eat anything."

Logan shifted, slightly uncomfortable with the familiarity, yet at the same time feeling oddly grateful for it.

"I haven't," he admitted. "This is very nice of you, Mr. Roman. Thank you."

Richard merely nodded, waving them both on their way.

But Andy wasn't quite ready to leave. "Dad, maybe I should see you to your room first."

Richard shook his head. "I'm not that fragile yet, Andy. I can still get around." He glanced at his watch and sighed. "This is usually the time of day I visit your mother, but I think she'll understand if I don't keep our appointment."

"You try going down that slope in this weather and I swear I'll have Silvio physically carry you off to bed," Andy told him.

"I'd laugh," her father responded, "but I know you're serious."

Andy never wavered. "You bet I am."

Leaning over, Richard kissed the top of her head. "I'll be good," he promised.

Frowning, she glanced in Logan's direction and said, "C'mon, let's go."

"HEY ALEX, LOOK what the cat dragged in," Andy called out the moment she reached her sister at the registration desk. "He'll be staying with us for the night."

Judging by her expression, her sister was trying to figure out if she was on the level or playing some sort of a prank.

"How did this happen?" Alex wanted to know, slanting one furtive glance in Logan's direction.

Andy raised and lowered her shoulders in an exaggerated shrug. "Seems that the only way to get to the freeway right now is to swim. Dad felt sorry for him—" she jerked her thumb at Logan "—and said to put MacArthur up in the Windsor Room."

She looked at Logan, thinking about everything that would happen if he and his firm were successful in what they planned to do.

"If it were up to me," she added, "you'd be spending the night in the broom closet."

"Still drier than outside," Logan told her stoically.

Andy stepped out of the way and allowed him access to the ledger.

Signing in, he accepted the key from Alex. "What do I owe for the room?" he asked, reaching for his wallet.

"Dad says not to worry about it," Andy informed him in a clipped voice. "C'mon, I'll take you to the dining area."

He was clearly having trouble accepting the act of kindness, in light of everything that had happened prior to that.

Good.

Belatedly, Logan fell into step beside her. "Why did he do that?"

Andy kept her face turned forward. Even

so, it was impossible to ignore the man. His presence seemed to seep into her senses. "Be more specific."

"Your father. He could have gone along with you about there not being any rooms available. I'd have no way of knowing if it was true or not."

She stopped walking for a minute to look at him. "Because my father is the kindest, most forgiving man I know. He would have put you up even if it meant giving you his room. He's just like that."

It didn't make sense to Logan. Acts of random kindness didn't happen in his world. "But I'm nobody to him."

"No, you're the guy who's trying to make him give up his life's work," Andy reminded him, struggling to keep her voice calm. "But he still would have put you up. It's just his nature. Selflessness is something that my father made a point of teaching all of us—but I'm a slow learner. Sit. I'll go see if there's anything to eat."

"Whatever is available will be fine," he called after her.

Andy kept walking.

Bursting into the kitchen, she crossed directly to Cris. "You're not going to believe this."

"Noah's outside, waiting for us to get into the ark?"

Andy shook her head "Even more unbelievable than that. Logan MacArthur is staying here, at the inn, thanks to Dad. He's in the dining room right now, waiting for me to bring him something to eat."

Cris blew out a breath. "Didn't see that one coming," she admitted. "Are you planning to throw it at him?"

"Don't tempt me," Andy warned. She took one quick look around. Lunch was technically over and things were being put away until dinnertime, which was fine with her. "If you don't have anything left—" she began, ready to leave the kitchen.

But Cris was more like their father than she was. "We do."

Andy fisted her hands at her side. "Drat," she muttered under her breath. Raising her voice she said, "Okay, Jorge, throw together whatever's left. Don't bother heating it up. Maybe even forgo including utensils on the tray."

Cris overrode her sister's instructions. "Heat up the stroganoff, Jorge." Turning toward Andy, Cris handed her a set of cutlery wrapped in a cloth napkin. "And you, you give this to Mr. MacArthur. Understand?" She looked into Andy's eyes.

Andy regarded the wrapped cutlery. "Sure you want to trust me with sharp objects around that man?"

"Andy, I know you're just fooling around," Cris said point-blank. "Nevertheless, this kind of talk is making me nervous."

Andy knew that Cris's being uptight in any way wasn't good for her unborn child. She sighed, backing off.

"Okay, in deference to the baby, I'll be on my best behavior. But if little he or she wasn't almost ready for their big premiere, there would be a happier ending to this story," Andy told her.

She deposited the napkin-wrapped utensils on a tray along beside a cup of coffee and the plate of stroganoff that Jorge had just heated.

Andy glanced down at the tray as she picked it up with both hands.

"You realize this is *not* the way to make the man go away," she said with an even deeper sigh.

"We're doing this because Dad wants us to," Cris reminded her.

"Yeah, yeah," Andy responded, resigned to the role her father had cast her in.

Jorge held the door opened for her.

"Thanks," she murmured as she passed through.

It was hard for her not to glare at Logan as she approached his table. "Here," she announced. "Your lunch."

"Smells good," Logan said, genuinely surprised that she had brought back anything other than dry bread and water.

Andy frowned. "I guess that means Cris forgot to put in the rat poison."

He unwrapped the utensils and placed the napkin on his lap. "Cris?"

"My sister. She runs the kitchen." One

of the people directly affected by the client he was representing.

"And your sister, Alex," he said, recalling the name she'd used earlier. "She's the one who runs reception?"

"For the most part, yes." Andy shifted from one foot to the other, restless. "Why are you asking? You didn't before."

"Before you weren't...people," he finally said for lack of a better way to describe his thinking.

"Yes, we were," Andy countered. "You just didn't bother to notice."

He couldn't, in all good conscience, argue that. "You're right. I had that coming," he admitted.

For a moment, she wanted to tear into him—but there was no point. Nothing would be accomplished and besides, her father wouldn't have wanted her to, and in the end, what he said went.

"Oh, and so much more," she told him, unable to hold her tongue. "Not that it matters." Still standing at the table, she leaned over slightly so that none of the inn's guests who might be passing by could hear her.

This was for Logan's ears alone. "We'll fill your belly, give you a place to sleep and tomorrow you'll still march off to that office of yours and work on the most efficient plan to get us thrown off our land."

She wasn't saying anything that she hadn't before, but for some reason, this time he actually took it in. Considered the justification of his client's actions, and for the first time he wondered how he personally felt about the job he had to do.

And for the first time in a very long time, Logan found himself not wanting to be alone.

"Would you sit down and have coffee with me?"

"Why?" she asked suspiciously. "I'd think that you'd be used to eating by yourself."

"I am," Logan admitted. "I...just don't want to right now."

There was something in the man's eyes, a glimmer of—what?

Loneliness?

Emptiness?

She supposed for lack of better words,

those would do to describe what she believed she was picking up from this high-priced-lawyer-without-a-heart.

Resigned, she agreed.

"Okay, I'll have some coffee." But she had to add, "Dad would want me to. That's why we're all so protective of him. He's like an innocent in the world. He believes there's good in everyone and if you focus on that, it'll surface, driving anything else into the background until it just disappears."

She stared at the high-priced lawyer.

He didn't even blink.

Good in everyone. What a joke.

She turned on her heel and headed to the kitchen. "I'll be right back."

"Something wrong?" Cris asked the second she saw her.

Andy frowned, responding with a half shrug. "He wants me to have coffee with him."

"Well, that's a hopeful sign, don't you think?"

Andy hadn't a clue. Right now, she just felt very confused.

"Maybe."

Positioning her cup under the industrial-sized coffee urn's spigot, she depressed the lever and filled the cup halfway, leaving room for a great deal of creamer. Adding that, she glanced at Cris over her shoulder. "Got any strychnine lying around?"

"Andy!"

Andy feigned disappointment at her sister's reaction. "You aren't any fun. You've really got to learn how to loosen up a little, Cris."

"I will—just as soon as you stop saying things like that," Cris countered. But Andy was already walking back to the dining room. "Try to behave," Cris called after her.

"I'll give it my best shot," Andy promised, pushing the door open and disappearing into the next room.

Logan had been watching the door, waiting for her return.

"I thought maybe you decided to make a break for it and leave through the back exit," he said when she sat opposite him.

"The inn is still in our name," Andy informed him. "So if anyone would be sneaking out and disappearing, it should be you."

Her answer made him smile a little. Most of the people he dealt with said one thing to his face, another behind his back. The trick was to read between the lines. But he didn't have to second-guess when it came to the woman sitting opposite him at the table. She spoke her mind—apparently every time she opened her mouth.

"Have you always been this direct?" Logan asked her.

"I'm the fourth sibling. If I didn't speak up, I would have gotten lost in the crowd a long time ago, especially since my oldest sister is a type A personality."

Logan paused for a moment, thinking over what she had just told him. "That would be the one I met at the front desk?"

"That would be the one you met at the front desk," she confirmed.

"And Cris? The one who runs the kitchen?"

"What about her?" Andy asked warily.

"Where is she on the personality spectrum?"

Andy studied him, surprised by the question. Was he actually asking, or was he just trying to get her to lower her guard around him?

"She's the second child. Stevi, the one who's getting married tomorrow is, by process of elimination, the third."

Why was MacArthur asking her questions about her family? Andy wondered again. He had to be up to something, right?

Good-looking or not, Andy trusted the man about as far as she could throw him.

Possibly even less than that.

"Leaving you to be the fourth," he concluded, coming full circle.

"Well, at least we know you can count up to four." Andy raised her coffee cup to her lips and then took a long, thoughtful sip.

What she still had to figure out, she told herself, was a way to activate the man's heart so that he would realize the impact losing the inn would have, not just on her family, but on so many others.

CHAPTER TWELVE

AFTER LOGAN HAD finished his lunch—
taking a pass on dessert and commenting
on how good the stroganoff had been—
Andy took the inn's reluctant guest to his
quarters.

The Windsor Room was located on the
second floor at the very end of the hall. It
was situated in a corner so that its win-
dows—and the views they provided—
opened on two sides of the inn.

Andy unlocked the door. Taking a step
back, she gestured for him to enter first.

"Isn't it supposed to be ladies first?"
Logan asked, remaining just outside the
room's threshold.

"I've seen the room before, you haven't.
It's your room for the night so you get to go
in first," she informed him, although she

had to admit—silently—that his manners did impress her just the tiniest bit.

Logan walked in and took his first look around the room. Accustomed to staying at hotels for business, it took him a moment to absorb the way the room was furnished.

The word *homey* jumped up at him out of nowhere. It was not a word he was in the habit of using, yet it was a very fitting description for the Windsor Room.

"Whose room is this?" he asked.

Andy thought she detected a thin thread of confusion in his voice. "Yours."

"I mean usually."

It was her turn to be a little confused. "Any guest who asks to stay in it. Why?"

This was awkward. He was usually very good at expressing himself. Never had a problem in the courtroom. "It just looks like someone's bedroom," he said slowly.

"That's the whole idea behind a bed and breakfast inn," Andy explained. "It's supposed to feel as if you're staying with family. With your great-aunt Ruth." She smiled.

He got the reference as soon as she said

it. He also picked up on the fact that for some reason, she thought he was clueless and wouldn't get her inside joke.

But of course he knew Ruth Roman had been the first in the family to open her home as an inn.

He scanned the room, murmuring absently, "I've never had family to stay with."

Why did Andy think he wouldn't do the necessary research to get his client's job done? Did she think he was a bad lawyer? Maybe she thought all lawyers were bad—a lot of people did.

Fingering the bedspread, he noted that it wasn't decor he would have chosen for his own sprawling house. But it did make him feel as if he was visiting a person rather than staying in an impersonal hotel room.

He supposed there was something to be said for that. Although he preferred an impersonal hotel room.

"Your parents never dragged you on an out-of-town, overnight trip to your grandparents' house or some random second cousin twice removed? Nobody?" she pressed, clearly having trouble believing him.

"No. Nobody." He wanted her to drop the subject, but one look at her told Logan that wasn't about to happen.

"What kind of vacations did they take you on?" she asked. She knew it wasn't any of her business, but that had never stood in her way before.

"I didn't go on vacations with them," Logan answered. "They did a lot of spontaneous globe trotting. Having me along would have proven to be too restrictive for them because of me being in school, so they left me with the housekeeper when I was very young. After that, there was boarding school."

"Wow, that's awful," she said, sympathy for the man beginning to stir in her.

This, she realized, went a long way to explain him. And being given this small glimpse inside him gave her hope.

"No," he contradicted her as he turned to face her. "That's practical."

It was her turn to contradict him. "No, that's awful."

Her eyes swept over Logan as if seeing him for the first time. Not as the man of privilege who was the hated emissary of the state, which was trying to take their home, but as a man whose parents had been too practical—his words—to spend their holidays with him. Had they not loved their only child? How could they have stood to be separated from him when he'd been a boy?

If she had children, she wouldn't want to let them out of her sight.

"You're beginning to make sense to me now," she told him.

"I had no idea that you were trying to make sense of me," Logan responded coolly.

"Human beings are supposed to make sense," she insisted. "All except for serial killers, of course, but you're not that."

Logan laughed shortly. "Well, thanks for ruling that out."

"No problem," she answered.

She chose to be unaffected by his sarcasm. She was beginning to understand that was his defense mechanism.

What he needed to thaw him out was someone with patience who would get him to come around and immerse himself in relationships with others, not just use people as pawns, as a means to an end.

An end that ultimately brought him no satisfaction that she could tell. She had never seen anyone so successful who seemed so unhappy about it.

It had been her intention to leave the moment she'd shown him to his room, but after what Logan had just told her, she felt compelled to stay with him a little while longer, maybe even attempt to chip away at his hard exterior to get to the person she had begun to believe was inside him.

She crossed to the large, multipaned window in front of her.

"On a clear day—when we have one of those," she qualified, "you can look out at the ocean and see for absolute miles. It makes you feel small, yet special at the same time."

Logan shrugged. That sounded like a contradiction to him but he was beginning to know better than to say so. "I'll take your word for it."

"And on this side," she continued, taking his hand and drawing him over to the window that was kitty-corner to the first one, "you can catch a glimpse of the main road as well as the ocean—again on a clear night."

Right now, the only thing that was visible were the sheets of rain coming down, blocking out anything that existed beyond the windowpanes.

"I guess I'll have to take your word for that, too," he said, checking out the window. "It really doesn't look like it's about to let up any time in the near future."

"That's why they call this the rainy season." She shrugged. "It's been so dry these past few years, I've forgotten what this could be like." Her mouth curved. "One winter, when I was a little girl, it felt like it had been raining every day for at least a month. I can remember wondering how I could go about becoming a mermaid in case I had to save my dad and my sisters."

He looked at her quizzically.

"You know," she continued, "dive in and pull them to safety if the water flooded everything."

"That's why you wanted to be a mermaid?" Logan asked. "Because you wanted to save your family from drowning?"

It seemed plausible to her. "Sure, what better reason was there?"

"Out of curiosity, how old were you?"

She thought for a minute. "Seven, maybe eight. Why?"

"No reason," he answered with a shrug, struggling to recall if he'd ever once dreamed of coming to his parents' rescue. If he'd ever had a dream about a flood, most likely he would've been the one treading water while his parents sailed away on the ark.

He was trying to find the root of this all-for-one-and-one-for-all attitude of Andy's. Granted, it wouldn't change anything he had to do, but maybe if he understood it, he'd be better equipped to make her and the rest of the Romans see the light of day. To get them to be practical.

Andy needed to get going. Tomorrow—and the wedding—would be here before she knew it. "Well, you know where the dining room is. Dinner is from five until eight."

He didn't feel like mingling. "No room service I take it?"

She shook her head. "Only if you're sick."

She had her hand on the doorknob and knew she should just go. There were a few more details she needed to see to regarding Stevi's wedding and she wasn't a last-minute person. She didn't want Stevi to have an anxiety attack, either.

Even so, something was making her linger here with this man a little longer. Maybe it was the image of a lonely little boy being left behind or sent off to boarding school because he got in the way of his parents' lifestyle. That had to have affected him.

She heard herself saying, "You know, the weather station is predicting another major storm rolling in tomorrow morning."

His eyes met hers. "Is that supposed to cheer me up?"

If she could just change his attitude, she

might, just might, find a way to turn him into an ally instead of an opponent.

She was willing to do whatever it took to save the inn. "What I meant was that if it turns out you can't leave tomorrow, you're welcome to attend Stevi's wedding."

Logan looked at her in surprise. "I'm sure your father would just love that, having me at his daughter's wedding."

"Actually," she said honestly, "he probably would. My father is the kind of man who, sooner or later—and it's usually sooner—makes friends with everyone he meets."

"There are the exceptions that prove the rule."

Was he saying that he planned to resist any and all attempts at friendship? Or didn't he think himself worthy of friendship?

"Oh, you're not as horrible as you think," she informed him.

"That's not what I meant."

She merely smiled as she left his room, murmuring, "Isn't it?"

Richard Roman's youngest daughter

closed the door and was gone before Logan could say anything in response.

LOGAN HAD EVERY intention of foregoing dinner. How many times had he worked straight through at the office, forgetting to eat, forgetting to go home?

But time moved differently when there was absolutely nothing to do, nothing to occupy his mind.

For all intents and purposes, he was marooned. The call he'd placed to one of the senior partners at the firm had abruptly turned into static five words into the conversation. The connection dissolved immediately after that.

The next call hadn't even gone through.

Neither had the third or fourth before he finally gave up, bouncing his cell phone off his bed in sheer frustration.

It landed on the floor, the blank screen mocking him.

It was around then that Logan became aware of another rustic touch. There was no TV in his room—not even a small, black-and-white, antiquated analogue set.

What in God's name did the people who stayed at this inn do to entertain themselves?

Checking his phone again—and hoping against hope—he found that he wasn't able to access his email. The rain was apparently blocking everything, including radio waves.

Logan took a small flashlight out of his briefcase and slipped it into his pocket. The way things were going, he figured a power outage was in their near future.

He might as well get something to eat while he could.

It took him a few minutes to retrace his steps to the small elevator that had been put in about a dozen years ago, as his tour guide had informed him on the way to the room earlier. Next to it were the stairs, and after a moment's debate, he decided he could do with the exercise.

The stairwell brought him to the first level, and just as he reached it an elderly woman as thin as a knife blade opened a door and stepped out.

Her gray eyes widened as she took in

the sight of him. "Back again, Mr. MacArthur?"

He didn't have a clue who the woman was. Yet she recognized him and knew his name.

"Yes," he replied, not knowing what else to say. Senior citizens made him uneasy. He couldn't relate to them, talk to them, unless they were in court, of course. This lady had to be in her 90s, he figured.

"Come to find out what makes us tick?" she asked as she looked at him intently.

"Excuse me?"

"Tick, Mr. MacArthur. You know, like a clock. Tick-tick-tick," she elaborated. "If you can find out what it is about this inn that draws so many people, perhaps you'll hold off giving this fine old place the ax."

Logan shook his head. He didn't have that sort of power—his boss didn't have that sort of power. "Not my call, ma'am."

The expression on the old woman's face told him she had different ideas.

"Don't underestimate yourself, my boy," she told him. "You could be the hero of Ladera by the Sea if you wanted to be."

Her tone brooked no argument.

"Let's just agree to disagree, Mrs.—?"

"Ms. Ms. Carlyle," she said with what could only be referred to as an impish smile. "I *am* right. Now, are you going in to dinner?"

"I might be," he responded.

"Coy," she noted. "I used to like that in a man. Now I find it just wastes my time and I have little enough of that left. Would you be so kind as to escort me into the dining room?"

It was a request she obviously did not expect to have turned down. He offered her his arm and said, "It would be my pleasure."

Ms. Carlyle smiled as she slipped her hand through the crook of his elbow. "Of course it would."

When he brought her into the room, she pointed out the table that was reserved for her. "That one."

Logan ushered her to it and held out the chair for her until she sat down. It was a slower process than he was accustomed to.

"Join me," she urged, taking hold of his

hand as he was about to leave to sit else-where.

"Excuse me?"

"You don't strike me as being hard of hearing, young man." Nonetheless, Ms. Carlyle repeated her invitation. "Join me. I sincerely doubt you've made any friends at the inn since you were last here."

He hesitated.

"Don't worry, Mr. MacArthur, I have no desire to proposition you," she assured him, with a very straight face.

Caught entirely off guard, Logan's mouth dropped open. Swiftly getting himself back under control, he cleared his throat.

"Nothing like that even crossed my mind," he told her.

"It didn't?" she asked, as if his words had fashioned themselves into a unique gem and she was examining it from all possible angles. "Pity," she lamented softly. "Because it did mine."

He could have sworn he saw a twinkle in the woman's eyes as she said it. Logan began to relax a little. He didn't get a lot of opportunity to practice his sense of humor,

but he wouldn't have been much of a lawyer if he didn't recognize and appreciate
humor in others. This woman had a very
dry wit.

"I suppose this will be filed under
missed opportunities," he told her.

When she smiled, *really* smiled, several
decades melted away.

Ms. Carlyle nodded. "I suppose so."

"WHAT'S HE DOING with Ms. Carlyle?" Cris
asked Andy as they stood watching the un-
likely couple at the older woman's table
from the door into the kitchen.

The second Andy had glimpsed Logan
escorting Ms. Carlyle to her table—and
then being roped into remaining—she'd
gravitated toward the door, curious. Was he
pumping the former school teacher for information? Or was it the other way around?
Ms. Carlyle, they had all learned, was not
to be underestimated.

"Entertaining her—I think," Andy said,
her eyes riveted on the pair.

"Maybe you should intervene, help her
out," Cris suggested.

"Ms. Carlyle can handle herself," Andy told her. "And maybe she can deliver a miracle."

"Well, now you've crossed the line between reality and fantasy," Cris said. What she knew to be on Andy's mind required a very large miracle.

"That's what we're going to need if we're ever going to get those people to keep their grubby little hands off the inn," Andy said with feeling. "Who knows, maybe we'll get a Christmas miracle. This is certainly the time for it."

Cris regarded her sister with awe. "I've never heard you talk this way."

"I've never been this desperate," Andy answered.

"In the meantime, someone needs to take their order," Cris pointed out. She looked around for Cheryl. "Where's Cheryl?" she asked Jorge.

"On break," he replied. Pausing, he wiped his hands on his off-white apron. "I think she's out back. Want me to go get her?"

"That's okay," Andy said. "I'll take their orders."

She was out of the kitchen before either Cris or Jorge could say anything.

CHAPTER THIRTEEN

"GOOD EVENING." ANDY flashed a bright smile at Ms. Carlyle, then kept it in place as she nodded at the older woman's table-mate. "What can I get you for dinner to-night?"

Logan studied her. "Are you the wait-ress here, too?"

"Food server," Andy corrected him automatically. "And I am anything I need to be to keep the inn running smoothly and our guests happy. That's the cardinal rule for everyone on the inn's staff," she added, then got back to the immediate business at hand. "Now, what'll it be?" she asked, looking at Ms. Carlyle.

As always, Cris had provided a choice of three meals. Two with meat and one that was strictly vegetarian.

Ms. Carlyle didn't need three choices.

She ordered her favorite, pot roast, along with a vegetable medley of carrots, peas and tiny red rose potatoes, quartered and sautéed.

"And I'd like a glass of white wine with that." The long-time guest handed Andy her menu. "I find it takes the chill out of my bones," she told Logan. "And before you say anything, yes, I know that red wine goes with the meal better than white, but I abhor red wine."

"I wouldn't presume to contradict you, Ms. Carlyle. I'll have the same," he told Andy, then added with a smile, "Including the white wine."

"Rebel," Andy murmured under her breath as she jotted the information down on her pad. When she glanced up at Logan, the look in his eyes told her that he'd heard her. "Be right back," she told the unorthodox duo.

"If you're wondering," Ms. Carlyle began without any preamble the moment Andy had disappeared into the kitchen, "Andrea's a very nice girl. She's the Roman daughter who got all the positive genes—bubbly and always good-natured."

Positive and good-natured, eh? Logan laughed softly. "I've noticed."

Ms. Carlyle seemed to sit up a little straighter, clearly prickling at his sarcasm. "Andrea is also very devoted, to her family and, of course, to the inn."

"I've noticed that, too," he acknowledged.

Ms. Carlyle gave her dinner companion a glare that had once inspired fear in the hearts of her students. "Then, young man, I am sure you've also noticed that these are good people. Especially their father," she said with emphasis. "There's no way of knowing how many lives he's saved."

Logan looked at her, confused. Had he missed something? "Excuse me? I'm afraid I don't follow."

"Ah, something you haven't 'noticed,' then," she said with a triumphant nod of her head. "He has this sixth sense about people. I've witnessed it more than once," she confided. "Richard just *knows* when someone is desperate, tottering on the edge. He takes them in, restores their dignity by having them work off their room and board and helps them get back on their feet. By the time they leave, they're facing a whole new life. That's because of Richard.

"Some, of course, cannot bring themselves to leave," she continued. "Like Dorothy, the housekeeper, and Silvio, the gardener. There were others," she recalled. "But if the inn goes, there won't be any more." She leveled a piercing look at her dining companion. "I certainly wouldn't want that on *my* conscience."

The one-sided conversation was temporarily placed on hold as Andy brought a large tray to their table.

Logan waited until she left before picking up the thread of their conversation. This time when he told the former elementary school teacher that it was out of his hands, he was aware of feeling just the slightest twinge of what could only be labeled remorse.

He did his best to ignore it.

SINCE HIS EARLY TEENS, Logan hadn't been able to sleep through the night, getting no more than about five hours of sleep.

There was always too much on his mind and his brain was always working, always reminding him of things he needed to remember.

Logan supposed stress was the main culprit. Even when he'd been a teen. He supposed the stress back then had first started when he'd had to adjust to living at a boarding school away from home.

These days the list of stressors went on and on.

He made the logical assumption that this night's sleep would be no different from any of the others.

But when he finally lay down in the queen-size bed with its Wedgwood-blue down comforter, he sank into the calming comfort.

He hadn't been prepared for a good night's sleep.

The last time he'd had seven hours it had been right after his appendectomy during his junior year in high school.

When Logan opened his eyes the following morning, he'd thought that it was the middle of the night. There was nothing to orient him. Rain was still blocking out everything, tirelessly and relentlessly coming down and oppressively cloaking everything just as it had when he'd laid down.

Logan was about to roll over and try to go back to sleep, but, a creature of routine, he checked his watch to see what time it was.

It was half past six.

It took a few seconds for the number to register.

Bolting upright, he scrambled out of bed, dragging the comforter behind him before he got himself untangled. His adrenaline pumping, he showered and was dressed and ready to leave in less than half an hour.

The problem was, Logan realized as he looked out of the window again, he had nowhere to go. It was even too early for breakfast. According to the hours he'd seen posted in the dining room, breakfast wasn't served until seven thirty.

Still, he really didn't feel like being in

his room. Homey though it was, it was still too much like solitary confinement, and the idea of that was certain to drive him crazy. So he went downstairs.

The moment he came to the first floor, he saw that he wasn't the only one up at this hour. Quite the opposite. The first floor was alive with activity. And then he remembered that one of the sisters—the one who wasn't pregnant and who wasn't Andy—was getting married.

Shirley. No, Stephanie. The one who was getting married was Stephanie.

He practically collided with Andy in the common room.

It figured, Logan thought, reflexively grabbing her by the shoulders to keep her from bouncing off his body.

"Morning," he said, immediately releasing her as if touching her burned his hands.

She felt as if her insides were scrambling. Her mind was going in four directions at once and organized chaos was the immediate result.

"Yes, it is," she acknowledged, "and I

don't have time to spare. Stevi's wedding is in less than five hours."

"Anything I can do to help?" Logan asked.

The offer surprised her. Maybe, just maybe, there was hope for the guy, and for the inn, yet.

"Can you make the rain stop?" she asked him very seriously.

He shook his head. "Sorry, I skipped that class in college."

She sighed deeply. "Just my luck. How about putting out folding chairs?"

"That class I took," Logan deadpanned.

"Great, then come with me," she urged, leading him in a different direction. "I've got close to a hundred chairs to put out—but just for the ceremony," she qualified. "I need to have most of them put away again before the dancing starts."

Logan followed her to the large closet just off the hall.

In her own way, she seemed to have everything under control. He'd always admired organization. "You've got this all pretty much plotted out, don't you?"

"Sure." She unlocked the closet and pushed the door all the way open to reveal quite a deep space. "Every little girl has some kind of dream wedding plotted out years ahead of time." When he looked at her quizzically, she added, "Okay, so this is a little rushed and a bit of a compromise. I wouldn't call it my dream wedding…or Stevi's…except that Stevi gets to wear the wedding dress. Now, if you want to talk, go find someone else," she advised. "I've got to keep moving."

"I'll put out the chairs," he told her in case she thought he was trying to get out of the job.

The huge smile she flashed him went straight to his gut, causing an unexpected tidal wave of emotions. He stood staring after her, trying to figure out what was going on.

Cris had gotten up early and made sandwiches and smoothies for the people pitching in to set up.

"This way you don't suddenly faint from hunger," she explained as she presented Logan with a choice of breakfast.

He picked the closest thing, a smoothie. "The rain hasn't really let up since yesterday. Is your sister really expecting a hundred people to show up?" he asked as he began taking light blue folding chairs out of the closet.

"Almost everyone who's going to be attending the wedding is already here," Cris told him. He paused to look at her. "Stevi invited the inn's guests to her wedding."

"Strangers?" he asked. Was this Stevi trying to fill up the common room with random bodies for some sort of an effect?

"Not really," Cris said. "A lot of the people staying here are repeats, people who come back year after year. Some of them have been doing it for a lot of years and can remember when we were little girls," she told him with a smile that was similar to Andy's. "That makes them almost like family."

Despite her explanation, Logan was having trouble wrapping his mind around a concept like that. His own family hadn't wanted to spend time together and here were people who could have been deemed to be strangers actually excited about witnessing one of the innkeeper's daughters getting married. They clearly regarded the young woman as one of their own despite having nothing in common except for memories of their stay at the inn.

It was, Logan concluded as he went to take out another set of folding chairs, definitely a very strange, strange place.

WHEN LOGAN FINALLY ran out of chairs, the communal atmosphere of the people working around him induced him to volunteer for something else.

Along with Cris's husband, Shane—and her live wire of a six-year-old son, Ricky—Logan helped set several long tables against the wall opposite a polished piano he'd noticed earlier.

Once the tables were covered with pearl-white tablecloths, they were ready to hold all the different dishes that Cris and Jorge were busy preparing for Stevi and Mike's buffet reception.

Everything, Logan noted silently, looked

as if it was humming along according to Andy's schedule.

And then it wasn't.

Andy answered a call on her cell phone just as she came out to check on the flower arrangement she had Silvio bring in earlier. Whatever else the man might have been in his home country, Logan thought, he definitely had an incredible green thumb in this one.

Logan's attention was drawn back to Andy when he heard her moan. The smile on her face disappeared as she asked, "Are you sure?"

He stopped working, giving her his full attention.

"Have you tried to use it? Oh, you just did. And you couldn't—?" She bit down on her lower lip, trying to come up with a viable alternative. "No, I understand. Of course you'll be missed," she said, "but I guess it really can't be helped. I wouldn't want you and your friends to take a chance on washing out to sea—or wherever. Thanks for calling and letting me know," she said. The next moment she terminated the call.

"You look like you just found out Christmas was being canceled this year. Is something wrong?" he asked.

Andy raised her eyes, the fog in her brain lifting ever so slightly. For the first time she realized that Logan was standing in front of her.

"In the grand scheme of life, no," Andy answered. "In this little microcosm of an existence, oh, most definitely."

When she said nothing further, Logan asked, "Am I supposed to guess what it is?"

"Everyone's going to know when Stevi walks down the aisle to Jorge playing his harmonica."

And everything had been going so well, too, she thought, frustrated.

Andy blew out a breath, trying to pull herself together. "That was Don Bradley calling—the man I hired to play the piano," she explained. "He and his band can't get here because Ladera is still an island."

Andy dragged her hand through her hair, trying to come up with some sort of a solution to this hiccup. "I can have music piped in for dancing, but I don't happen to have a CD or anything like that with the wedding march on it. And we still have no Wi-Fi connection on our computer. Most likely, Jorge doesn't know how to play it on his harmonica."

Although she was talking out loud, she was basically talking to herself and not the man next to her.

Exasperated, she looked up at Logan. "It just won't be the same without the piano," she complained.

Logan glanced over his shoulder at the piano he'd noticed earlier. "Is that thing tuned?" he asked.

Although she was looking at him, her mind was miles away, searching for an alternative.

"What?" And then his question registered. "Oh, yes, it is. I had it tuned last week. It doesn't really get played much anymore. Actually, hardly ever." She paused, then added in a softer, sentimental voice, "It was my mother's. She liked to play, especially on warm summer evenings.

Whenever I hear it, it reminds me of her. It reminds *all* of us of her." Andy shrugged, pulling herself together. "I guess I'll just find a way to improvise."

Walking away, her mind going in four directions at once as she searched for a way to break the news to Stevi about this latest curveball they had been thrown, she didn't hear it at first.

Quite honestly, the sound didn't register with her brain until she had gone almost halfway across the floor toward reception.

Even when it registered, she was certain that she was just imagining it. But then the tempo sped up, adding a jazzy little riff to the music.

Andy's eyes widened as she turned toward the piano.

Stunned, she hurried back across the floor, weaving in and out between the chairs. Andy never took her eyes off the piano and the person sitting on the bench, playing.

MacArthur.

Logan MacArthur was playing a popular

song on her mother's piano. And sounding incredibly professional.

She would have said she was hallucinating except that, judging by their expressions of appreciation, everyone around her was hearing it, too.

"You play?" she asked, dropping onto the bench beside him.

"A little," Logan allowed. "One of the things my parents insisted on was that my right brain was as developed as my left brain. So they made me take lessons from the time I was four until I was shipped off to boarding school. Even after that, I was required to keep up with my lessons. And I did, for a while."

When he stopped the lessons, it was his way of rebelling against the parents who hadn't had any time for him.

"Can you play the wedding march?" Andy put the question to him eagerly, holding her breath as she waited for an answer.

"I think I can find it on the keyboard," Logan told her, picking out the notes. It took him two attempts. On the third try, he was successful.

"That's it," Andy cried. "You did it! You're a life saver!"

Thrilled, exuberant, Andy threw her arms around Logan. That part she remembered. But how she wound up kissing him she really wasn't clear on.

All she knew was that, at the moment, it seemed like the right thing to do.

CHAPTER FOURTEEN

WHAT ARE YOU DOING? Are you out of your mind? Piano player or not, this guy's still the enemy!

Andy was determined not to lose face despite the compromising position she had just put herself in.

Pulling her head back, she tried to cover up for having kissed him by making light of it.

"Sorry," she apologized, "I guess I got a little carried away there."

The woman had caught him completely off guard and there were no two ways about it, the youngest of Roman's daughters packed quite a wallop.

Enough to get him really thinking about the direction his life was headed in. Among other things.

"I guess I play better than I thought I

did," Logan said. And then he grew serious. "But you don't have anything to apologize for."

"Is this the latest way of auditioning musicians?" a deep male voice behind them asked.

Startled, Andy turned in her seat—and then smiled. "Call it more of a spur of the moment thing," she answered. "Logan MacArthur, this is my brother-in-law, Wyatt Taylor—Alex's husband. Wyatt, Logan," Andy said, gesturing from the man she had known for most of her life to the man she'd only known for less than a month.

Wyatt leaned forward, shaking the other man's hand. It was obvious that he was trying to place Logan's name and remember if he was supposed to be familiar with it. And then it came to him.

"Aren't you that lawyer who's representing the state?" he asked as everything clicked into place for him. Alex had asked him to contact his lawyer friend to fight this guy in court.

Wyatt's eyes narrowed. If this was the

enemy, what was Andy doing kissing the man?

"Right now, he's the piano player keeping Stevi's wedding from becoming a disaster," Andy informed Wyatt. "Tomorrow he'll be that lawyer. Today he's a pianist."

Wyatt, she knew, was almost as attached to the inn as she and her sisters were. Every summer, like clockwork, he and his dad, her own father's lifelong best friend, came to spend their vacations here. Wyatt's parents had split up because of his father's globe-trotting career as an investigative journalist, and while Wyatt's address for some of the year involved a New York City zip code, he really considered Ladera by the Sea his home.

He'd once confided to her that all his best memories were here, not to mention the fact that his father was laid to rest here in the Roman family cemetery. A screenwriter of no small renown, Wyatt had already told her he was prepared—not to mention willing—to fight for the inn no matter what it took—or what it cost.

"So make nice, Wyatt," Andy concluded,

patting her brother-in-law's arm. "We need him—for now."

Wyatt laughed, shaking his head. "You're getting as bossy as your oldest sister," he said. "I'd watch that if I were you." Wyatt rolled his eyes heavenward. "I don't think I could take two of you like that."

"Fair enough—just do as I say and there won't be any trouble," she said, managing to keep a straight face.

"*Just* like Alex," he said with a huge sigh.

The next moment, the time for conversations, serious and otherwise, had passed as a high-pitched voice called out for him. "Wyatt!"

Hearing his name called, Wyatt looked around, turning in the general direction he thought the summons had come from.

"I believe that was your master's voice," Andy teased, then advised more seriously, "I'd go before she becomes surly if I were you."

Wyatt lingered just a moment longer. Long enough to share a lament. "I can't wait until this pregnancy is over," he confided. "The way she is now makes her seem like she was a pussycat then."

Pulling his shoulders back like a man about to propel himself headfirst into a battle, Wyatt went off in search of his wife.

"I'll second that," Andy murmured under her breath.

"Is she having a hard time of it?" Logan heard himself asking.

It was hard to tell who was more surprised at the question—him or Andy. He wasn't given to personal chit-chat, especially not about absent parties.

Something had definitely changed with him, Logan thought.

"She isn't, we are," Andy answered. And then she amended her words. "That's not fair, I guess. It's just that, in comparison to Cris, Alex comes off less than sterling in her approach to motherhood-to-be."

"What do you mean?" he asked, finding himself being reeled in.

"Cris never complained about being nauseous, or her feet swelling or any of the rest of all those wonderful things that come along with pregnancy. Alex, on the other hand, feels compelled to issue daily up-dates on all the different ways she's uncom-fortable. Sometimes *twice* daily."

He could see how that might get a little old after a while. "When are they due?"

She didn't have to pause to think. She knew the answer by heart now. They were in countdown phase and she kept track of the days.

"End of the month, give or take."

He stared at her incredulously. "Both of them?" he asked.

Andy nodded her head. That was some-thing she was *not* looking forward to.

"Yup. It should be fun," Andy said sarcastically. "Especially if this weather doesn't cooperate."

He immediately thought of his own pre-dicament. "You mean like the freeways being inaccessible?"

She was thinking more along the lines of the doctor not being able to get to her sisters in time. The idea sent a cold shiver down her spine.

"Don't even go there," Andy said, closing her eyes. When they popped open again the next moment, she got to her feet quickly. "Okay, enough resting. I've still got a wedding to pull together. You," she said, giving Logan her final instructions, "be sure to make yourself available at noon. I'm going to need you to play the wedding march at twelve o'clock sharp."

He already got that part. "What about afterward?"

Andy looked at him, not following his drift. "Afterward?"

"Yes, afterward," he repeated. "I'm assuming the band was going to play at the reception, as well. Right?"

She had already worked out that particular problem. "Don't worry about that. I've got it covered. I can plug speakers into my MP3 player and give the guests plenty of music to dance to. You're off the hook after the wedding march," she told him cheerfully.

The next moment, Andy disappeared into the sea of chairs and people, leaving Logan looking after her and feeling as if he had been hit by a hurricane or some other force of nature.

The woman, he thought, his mind drifting back to the way her lips had felt against his, should come with a warning label issued by the Surgeon General.

LOGAN DIDN'T SEE the woman he was swiftly coming to think of as *the little dictator* until just before the wedding was to begin.

He didn't recognize her at first. The Andrea Roman he was acquainted with wore sandals, jeans and pullovers. She kept her hair pulled back and her makeup at a minimum. The woman who approached him was wearing four-inch heels and a blue-gray dress that hugged her like an old friend who was afraid to let go. The dress also stopped about six inches short of her knees, giving any observer the illusion that she had legs from here to eternity. Her hair was worn loose, a golden frame for her face.

Andy crossed to him quickly, double-checking that he was still here and still ready to play. Coming closer, she noticed the rather strange expression on his face. It

MARIE FERRARELLA   255

caused her to look down at her dress. But nothing was amiss as far as she could see.

"Something wrong?" she asked him.

Logan roused himself and said, "No, why?"

This was *not* the time to give in to old insecurities, she silently lectured herself. "Well, for one thing, you're looking at me as if I was wearing my dress inside out."

A smile of pure appreciation began to slowly move across his lips. "That's not why I'm looking at you," he assured her.

The way Logan said it had her suddenly fighting a blush.

"Okay, then," Andy announced, deliberately clearing her throat to buy herself a little time. "I think we're all ready to go. You can start playing the minute I go through those back double doors." She pointed to them. "When they part again a minute later, Stevi will be walking through."

Centering herself—her mind doing one last rapid inventory to make sure everything was set—Andy drew in a deep breath and then let it out again very slowly.

She was ready.

"Okay, let's do this," she told Logan just before she hurried away.

Logan didn't take his eyes off her until she disappeared. She was just as enticing leaving as she was approaching.

AFTER KNOCKING AND hearing a rather breathless "Come in," Richard opened the door and peeked into the room that was located right off the Common Room. For the purposes of today, the guestroom had been converted to the bride's room. Rather than walk through the length of the inn to get from her bedroom to the room where she was to be married, everything that Stevi was going to need to transform her into a bride—dress, make up, etc.—had all been arranged here for her by Andy and Dorothy.

"They're about to start, Stevi." Richard's voice hitched a little as he drank in the sight of her. The wedding dress that his wife had worn all those years ago still looked timeless. It fit Stevi as if it had been made for her. "My goodness but you are beautiful," he said, his voice brimming with emotion.

"Thank you." Stevi turned away from the floor-length mirror to smile at her father. And then she paused. "Dad, are those tears?"

"I plead the fifth," he replied.

Those were tears she saw shimmering in her father's eyes. "You think you'd be used to this by now." After all, he'd already given away two of his daughters.

"It's not something you get used to," he told her. "Giving your girls away." He took in the sight of her and felt his heart being tugged a little more. "Your mother would have loved to have seen you in her wedding gown."

"She did," Stevi told him. "I played dress up in it once when I was a little girl." Stevi grinned as she smoothed down her train. "As I recall, the gown was locked up and put away in the attic after that."

Pausing, Stevi cocked her head, listening for a second. "I think they're playing our song, Dad," she said. Turning, she took one last look at herself in the mirror to make sure everything was in place.

Ricky popped in.

"Ricky, what are you doing here?" Richard asked.

"Mommy said I should help Aunt Stevi with her train. I didn't know you had a train in here, Aunt Stevi." Decked out in his best suit and looking as if he was going to be scooped up and placed on top of the wedding cake at any moment, Ricky shifted uncomfortably as he looked around the room. "I don't see a train." He raised his small face up to his grandfather. "Where is it?"

"The back of a bride's dress is called a train, Ricky," Richard explained.

"Why? It doesn't look like a train."

"You're absolutely right," Stevi agreed. "It's just one of those things that make no sense, but everyone accepts. But I do need someone big and strong to hold the end of it off the ground so I can walk better. Think you can do that for me?"

Ricky bobbed his head up and down. "Uh-huh." As he picked up the edge of it, he said in an unusually shy—for him— voice, "Aunt Stevi, you look pretty."

She kissed the top of his head. "Thank

you. You make me feel pretty." She took in a deep breath to try to subdue the butterflies in her stomach. "Ready, gentlemen?" she asked.

Richard put his elbow out, allowing her to slip her arm through it. "Ready," he answered.

"Ready!" Ricky shouted.

"Then let's go," she said.

Richard guided his daughter out of the room.

"You're here," Andy declared, all but colliding with Stevi in her hurry to get things moving. "Perfect. Keep moving," she instructed, getting out of their way.

Everyone stood up as they entered.

ANDY COULDN'T REMEMBER the last time she had felt this pleased with herself. The wedding had gone off without a single hitch. The music was perfect.

Logan had played even better than she could have hoped for.

Unlike Alex and Cris—and her father, as well as Dorothy—she had stoically remained dry-eyed throughout the entire ceremony.

Even so, what she felt on the inside was another matter. Andy could still feel tears welling up when she remembered the moment Stevi stepped into the room and how Mike's eyes had lit up.

She fought back the tears again.

It was, to her, the official end of her childhood—not that she would ever have said as much to any of her sisters. But they had each crossed that threshold, the one that took them from carefree childhood to a life of adult responsibilities.

And she had been forced to follow, not wanting to remain in childhood alone.

The new world required serious thought, serious action. And once there, there was no going back as far as she could see.

She fought back the sadness.

Right after the ceremony, Jorge had joined Logan and together the two men had played the first set as a piano and harmonica duet, even though she had volunteered her MP3 player the moment the chairs were cleared away.

When the pair finally took a break, she insisted on replacing them with her sound system. "So that you can go, eat, mingle and enjoy yourselves," she told them.

Jorge didn't have to be told twice, but Logan seemed somewhat reluctant to abandon the piano.

"I was enjoying myself," he confessed, surprising himself as well as her.

"Enjoy yourself differently," she said.

She'd placed her father in charge of the music from there on in, thinking that this way, he wouldn't tire himself out but he could still make a major contribution to the celebration.

She had all the bases covered, Andy congratulated herself as she looked around the common room.

The music filling the air the next moment was a timeless love song.

Logan got up from the piano bench. "Since I'm not playing anymore, do you have any objections to my dancing?" he asked.

She thought it was an odd question. "No, of course not. That's why I said I was replacing you with my sound system. So you could enjoy yourself."

"Okay," he said. He held out his hand to her. "Then may I have this dance, Ms. Roman?"

Andy felt her heart skip a beat, then slip into double time.

She didn't want to dance with him. It was too risky. She had an uneasy premonition that her thoughts and her feelings would come to a parting of the ways, though, once his arms were around her.

"I don't dance very well," she demurred, thinking that would be enough to put him off.

"Lucky thing all this song requires is a pulse and the ability to sway."

Taking her by the hand, he led her to the section of the floor that had been reserved for dancing.

Most of the folding chairs had been collected and put back into the utility closet, he noticed and wondered who she'd commandeered to do that. He'd just naturally assumed that, since he was the one who had put them out in the first place, it would be his responsibility to gather them up as well. But Andy had managed to outmaneuver him.

"Well, if you're bound and determined to have me step all over your feet, let's do this and get it over with," she said, as if she was about to face a firing squad.

Logan laughed. "You really have the most picturesque way of saying things. I hate to break it to you but I don't think you have much of a future in an advertising agency."

"Among other things, I was an English major in college."

"An English major," Logan repeated. He could see her doing that, getting lost in words for their own sake. "To what end?"

She lifted her shoulders in a vague shrug. "Beats me," she admitted. "I also have enough undergraduate credits to qualify as premed—or an accounting major."

His admiration of her went up another notch. "When you were a kid, exactly what did you want to be when you grew up?"

"An adult," she quipped.

Logan's blue eyes swept over her. "Well, you certainly have accomplished that goal."

The compliment warmed her more than she thought it would. Andy smiled.

"You know, you're not half bad when you give yourself a chance."

He supposed he had come on as humorless and dour during their first couple of encounters. "You mean when I'm not twirling my moustache or tying Little Nell to the railroad tracks?"

"When you're not crushing dreams," she told him pointedly.

His eyes searched hers for a moment. "That isn't exactly part of my job description," he answered.

"Nonetheless, that doesn't change the fact that when you're successful that's what you wind up doing."

"I think you should know this is the first expropriation I've ever been involved in."

"Exprop—" Andy choked on the word and tried not to tighten her grip on the man to the point of pain.

The next moment, she sighed. "Sorry, I promised myself there'd be no shop talk today. You did me a huge favor by stepping up." She knew that he could have just as easily said nothing. He didn't have to tell her he played the piano. "And on behalf of my sister, I thank you."

"Don't thank me, thank my parents. They're the ones who insisted I take those endless lessons."

She recalled what he had said about them earlier. She'd gotten the definite impression that Logan was estranged from them.

Even so, something prompted her to ask, "When did you last talk to them?"

He thought for a moment. "I don't know. What year is it again?"

Andy stopped dancing and stared at him. "You are kidding, aren't you?"

Very gently, he coaxed her into moving again and following his lead.

"If that's what you'd like to believe, then, yes, I'm kidding."

"You really haven't talked to your parents in a year?" she asked, stunned. She couldn't imagine what that was even like.

Another song began when the last one

ended. It was another slow number so Logan just continued dancing with her.

"Years," he corrected. "My parents and I haven't spoken in years."

"Years?" Andy echoed in disbelief, her eyes widening.

How could he have allowed that to happen? She thought of herself in that situation and was unable to picture it.

He couldn't help thinking that Andy looked rather adorable right now. And he supposed part of him found it touching that she seemed to care that he was out of touch with the couple who had given him life. Even if he didn't. "That's right."

She couldn't make herself believe that this didn't bother him, that he hadn't attempted to rectify the breech.

"By choice?"

He looked at her as the beat picked up. Going with it, Logan swung her around. "I believe it's mutual."

That was pain in his eyes, she was sure of it. He was trying to be blasé, to act as if it didn't matter, but he just couldn't be that removed, that cold inside. She refused to accept that.

"Oh, Logan, I'm so sorry."

A flippant comment rose to his lips, but then he looked at her and it faded away. "You really mean that, don't you?"

"Of course I mean it," she responded with feeling. "I can't imagine not talking to my father—or my sisters—for a day much less years. Really?" she asked one last time, hoping he'd been exaggerating.

But he hadn't been. "Really."

The lack of family contact genuinely seemed to bother her.

"Let's talk about something else," Logan suggested. Before she could protest or ask him any more questions about his personal life—or lack of it, he told her, "You throw a really mean wedding."

She let his sad attempt to divert her ride.

"Thank you." She looked around the floor at the other couples dancing. She saw Stevi laughing at something Mike had just said to her and her heart warmed all over again. "I couldn't have done it without help," she replied. "It's not the wedding I would have wanted for Stevi, but at least we're getting through it without any major incidents."

"Like what?" he asked.

"The lights haven't gone out on us," Andy pointed out, thinking of all the different areas that had gone dark during the storm.

The words were no sooner out of her mouth than the lights began to flicker. They did that twice, then suddenly, the lights and the music came to an abrupt, jarring halt.

The common room fell into darkness.

"You were saying?" Logan asked, still holding on to her as if they were dancing.

"That I should never take anything for granted and never, ever say things out loud. It's like asking to be cursed. Shane?" she called, raising her voice. "Shane, can you turn on the generator, please?"

When she received no answer from Shane after calling to him the second time around, Andy began to grow anxious.

CHAPTER FIFTEEN

SHE WAS AWARE of Logan letting her go. And then Andy saw the thin, long beam of light suddenly appearing right next to her.

For a second, it startled her.

"I know you don't glow in the dark, so what is that?" she asked Logan.

"High beam flashlight," he told her. "I put it in my pocket before the ceremony because I had an uneasy feeling we might need it."

We. Did that mean he was aligning himself with her and her family? Or was he just lumping them together only for the duration of the storm and once it was over, he and she would go back to their separate corners?

Not knowing really bothered her.

This wasn't the time to get philosophical, she told herself sternly. This was the time to find the generator and kick-start it so her sister's wedding wouldn't end with people getting trampled trying to get out.

"Where's the generator?" Logan asked.

"It's in the basement," she answered, then beckoned for him to follow her. "C'mon, I'll show you. Hang in there, everybody," she declared in a louder voice. "We'll have the lights back on shortly." She discreetly kept her crossed fingers out of sight. The look on Logan's face when she caught it in the moving beam of the flashlight told her that he'd seen.

Once they were out of the common room, she had Logan shine his high-powered flashlight in front of her so she could find the basement door.

In the dark, it seemed to take forever, but eventually, they located it. Andy reached for the handle only to have Logan move her out of the way. She looked at him quizzically, then realized when he pulled the door open that he was being chivalrous. Again.

The stairs leading down to the basement were steep and narrow. Even with the beam lighting all the way down, it was still pretty dark in her opinion. Making a misstep was a very real possibility.

"This is the part in the movie where the monster pops up," she murmured under her breath.

She slanted a glance toward Logan, fully expecting to hear him laugh. To his credit—and her surprise—he didn't.

"I'll go down first," he volunteered, carefully snaking his way until he was ahead of her. "Do you believe in monsters?" he asked casually as he began to make his way down the creaky steps.

"No, not when the lights are on," Andy said a bit quickly, then confessed, "but I do have an overactive imagination."

"That would be fueled by the English major in you," he guessed.

It seemed like as good a reason as any. "I suppose," she allowed.

She hung on to the banister until she reached the last step. Logan's flashlight gave life and depth to shadows and illuminated all sorts of confusing shapes in all sizes.

"Did you happen to see Shane before the

lights went out?" she asked Logan. She was trying not to be concerned, but it wasn't working. "It's not like him not to answer."

"Maybe his wife got tired and he took her to their room," Logan suggested.

They were picking their way through a pile of boxes and containers. On the wall shelving stood a myriad of objects that had once been considered precious treasures but now appeared to be just so much random junk. It had been a long time since anyone had cleaned out the basement.

As Logan narrowly avoided tripping over a sealed carton, he glanced over his shoulder at her. "Did you ever consider having a garage sale?"

"Very funny."

"I'm being serious."

She rolled her eyes. That sounded like a quick solution—but in reality, it wasn't.

"First, I'd have to go through everything. These don't just belong to my sisters and me, there are keepsakes here that belonged to past generations. You know this—the inn has been in the family for over a hundred and twenty years. That translates into a *lot* of accumulating."

"Some of this could be valuable," he grudgingly agreed.

"Could be *invaluable* is more like it."

He was having a hard time finding the generator through the clutter.

"Right now, what would be invaluable would be finding that generator." Logan spared her a glance. "You're sure it's down here?"

A generator as back-up power for a place the size of the inn wasn't exactly something that could be misplaced.

"I'm sure," she answered with finality. "It's just hard finding it in the dark."

"No argument," he said in complete agreement. "But if you're sure it's here and not, say, in the attic, we'll find it eventually," he said, circumventing a rather large wooden rocking horse. "It couldn't have gotten up and walked away—unless of course the monster took it." Logan grinned. "You can never tell with a monster."

Andy heard the grin rather than saw it. "Not funny."

"Actually, it is. But I'll stop," he promised.

As he spoke, he made wide arcs with his flashlight, trying to find some sign of the illusive generator. Apparently the basement ran the length of the entire inn. This could take hours, he thought.

"Wait, is that it?" He steadied the flashlight, slowly panning the beam over his discovery.

"Has to be," Andy answered excitedly. "It doesn't look like anything else."

He couldn't resist one final jab. "Could be the monster, being a shape-shifter."

"Remind me to pummel you to the ground once the lights are back on."

Playing the flashlight all along the generator's side, he looked for the switches to get the inn operating.

Because of the tight space, Andy was forced to stand behind him rather than next to him. She shifted from foot to foot impatiently.

"Anything?" she asked, angling to see around him.

"I'm working on it," Logan told her. "Believe it or not, I wasn't born operating a generator. This is my first one." And he was throwing every switch one at a time and hoping for the best.

"Right now your honesty doesn't exactly fill me with confidence."

The basement was still encased in darkness except for the beam coming from his flashlight.

"Sorry," he bit off absently, wondering if there was some sort of configuration he should have been trying. "Have you got experience with it? Would you like to try?"

"What I'd like is for you to make that thing turn the lights on," she said, frustrated.

No sooner had she said the words than, just like that, the light switch she'd fumbled with to no avail before they came down worked and brought up the overhead lights.

She fervently hoped that the same was happening upstairs.

Logan released the breath he'd been holding. "You were saying?" he asked, turning. He appeared very satisfied with himself.

"This was tantamount to your saying let

there be light," she acknowledged. "If you can do that, why can't you make the rain stop?" she asked him.

"Never satisfied," he said with a shake of his head. "One miracle at a time, Andy. One miracle at a time."

He looked back at the generator, checking to see if there was anything else he should be attending to. He was basically going by instinct rather than any sort of an inherent knowledge of these things. The generator seemed to be working, which as far as he was concerned, was all that really mattered.

Shane would be able to take it from here, Logan figured, more than willing to hand over the responsibility to the man. Once they found him.

"Okay, I guess we're done here." He glanced around the area one last time. With the lights on, the basement appeared to be completely overloaded with paraphernalia. "There really is a *lot* of stuff down here."

Andy's only response was to say, "You think this is something, you should see the attic."

He looked at her for a long moment. If he won the case for the state and the way it seemed he was certain that he would, Andy and her family were going to have a great deal to go through in what could be a limited amount of time.

But for now, he decided it was best not to mention that.

"Why don't we go back upstairs and find out what happened to Shane," he urged. When he saw her surprise, he could guess what she was thinking. "I'm beginning to learn that you can't seem to relax in any manner unless you know everyone in your family is safe and sound. If any of them is out of sight, I think you immediately assume they're neither safe nor sound."

"That's not true," Andy protested, then added in a smaller voice, "Exactly."

Logan laughed. Putting his flashlight back in his pocket, he took her hand and said, "Let's go."

The stairs seemed less narrow to her on the way up than they had on the way down.

The door to the basement was located in an out-of-the-way corridor that ran the length of the back of the inn. For the most part, the suites here were newer than the ones at the center of the first floor, added by Shane. The project had been responsible for bringing him to the inn in the first place. It seemed only fitting that he and Cris had turned part of the addition into their own living quarters.

A gut feeling made Andy pause before heading down the new wing.

"Something wrong?" Logan asked.

If she was wrong, Logan was going to think she was a paranoid idiot. "Probably not."

"But?"

She didn't want him here as a witness to her paranoia. "Why don't you go on back and join the reception? I'm sure everyone wants to thank you, especially Stevi and my Dad," she encouraged. "You're the hero of the day, bask in it."

She didn't fool him. "And what are you going to be doing while I'm basking?"

"I'll be checking out a gut feeling." She hesitated before elaborating when he didn't move. "I just want to satisfy myself that Cris and Shane aren't in their room."

He had a feeling that was exactly where they were. "Like I said, maybe she got tired and he's just being the good husband."

"And that's great," Andy agreed. "But maybe Cris being tired isn't the reason they're not at the reception."

It didn't take a rocket scientist to figure out what was going on in Andy's head. "You think she's having the baby, don't you?"

Andy nodded vigorously.

"Well, now you've got me curious." At this point, they were standing directly in front of the couple's living quarters. "What are you waiting for?" He gestured at the door. "Knock!"

She did. At first softly, then, as her concern became more pronounced, Andy knocked harder. "Shane, are you in there?" she asked. "Is Cris okay?"

The door opened and an ashen Shane stood just inside the room.

"She's having the baby, Andy. But the roads are still washed out so I can't drive her to the hospital and I can't even get through to the doctor." He looked like a man at the end of his rope—and said as much. "I don't know what to do."

Ordinarily Shane was not a person who panicked. But this was different. This involved the life of the person he loved most in the whole world as well as that of his unborn child.

"What we do," Andy told her brother-in-law as calmly as she could, "is help bring this baby into the world." She glanced around the sitting area. "Where's Ricky?"

"I left him at the reception with your father," Shane answered.

"Good, they'll keep each other occupied." With one problem down, Andy began making a list in her head. "Okay, I need to wash my hands," she told him just before she strode toward the bathroom.

Shane looked relieved. "You've done this before?"

"I've witnessed it once before," Andy corrected, not wanting to give him any false impressions. "I had a friend at the university who was a single expectant mom.

She asked me to be her coach because the baby's father had decided he wanted no part of either of them. I was with her in the hospital when she gave birth. Mostly she held on to me so hard she almost broke my hand. Anyway, Cris will do the work and she's done this before. We're just the cheering section."

Drying her hands, she went into the bedroom and smiled at Cris. "Looks like you won't be making Belgian waffles tomorrow morning."

Cris gritted her teeth as she struggled past another contraction.

"You get me through this," she told Andy, "and you'll get Belgian waffles for life."

"Best offer I've heard so far," Andy told her sister, relieved that Cris was able to joke in this moment. "Okay, how far apart are the contractions?"

Cris couldn't answer immediately. One of the contractions had seized her, stealing her breath away and tying the rest of her up into a hard knot.

It wasn't until the pain subsided, moving out like a wave on the beach, that she could finally answer. "They're not apart at all. They're dovetailing into one another."

Andy shut her eyes briefly. What on earth did she know about giving birth? Wouldn't Alex be better able to help right now? But, she realized as soon as that thought occurred to her, Alex wasn't here. She was.

"Sounds like showtime to me," she told her sister as cheerfully as she could. Squeezing Cris's hand she said encouragingly, "You've been through this once before. This time around should be a piece of cake."

"The *last* time was a piece of cake," Cris corrected. "This time, it feels more like it's a stale, hard loaf of French bread."

Her eyes widening, Cris dug her heels into the mattress and raised herself up in an attempt to be somewhere the pain wasn't.

She failed.

Cris squeezed her eyes shut as another wave of pain washed over her.

"Logan, go find Dorothy," Andy said. "Tell her to come as quickly as she can.

We need help. Unless you can find some kind of nurse or doctor among those guests gathered for the wedding!"

"If I can't find her and there's no health-care professionals, how about one of your sisters?" he suggested.

Andy shook her head. "One's pregnant, the other's a bride. Bring me Dorothy," she repeated. "Go, go!"

The next moment, Logan hurried out.

"What do you want me to do?" Shane asked. He wasn't accustomed to feeling so helpless.

"Get behind Cris's head on the bed." She waited until he was in position. "Now lift her shoulders up so that you're propping her up into a sitting position. That's it," she told him, nodding. "And you," she addressed Cris, "I figure that all this is coming back to you right about now."

Cris nodded. "In…glorious…*color*!" she gasped just before she bit her lip.

"Don't bite your lip. You're liable to pierce it. Not an attractive look for a mother of two."

Cris's answer wasn't anything remotely intelligible.

"You made one beautiful baby," Andy reminded her sister. "So you know how it's done. It's time to push out another, honey." She saw the frantic way Cris was twisting on the bed. "You can do this, Cris, you know you can."

"You've…got…more…faith…in…me… than…I do."

"Well, the alternative is to stay pregnant forever and I'm thinking you'd rather not go that route. So you're going to push, right?"

"Right!" Cris screamed as, with Shane propping her up again, she leaned forward as far as she could. Eyes tightly shut, she focused on bearing down as much as she could. The grunting grew louder and louder.

Andy gave it to the count of ten in her head, then ordered her sister to relax.

Shane withdrew his hands from her back and Cris collapsed against the pillows.

"Is it…too…late to…change…my mind?"

she asked, her voice up at the end of the sentence.

"I'm afraid so, Cris. The only way out of this is to have that baby." She looked at Shane who was the picture of impotent concern. "You're doing fine. You both are."

At least she hoped this was going fine. What did she really know? She took a very deep breath.

Shane leaned forward and pressed a kiss to his wife's damp forehead.

"It's not easy watching someone you love go through this kind of pain," Andy said. She saw that Cris had begun propping herself up on her elbows again. "Ready?"

"Ready," Cris gasped.

"All right, here we go," Andy declared, then ordered Cris to "Push!"

CHAPTER SIXTEEN

EMOTION FLOODED THOUGH Andy. She could feel perspiration gathering along her hairline and there was a trickle sliding down her spine. And she wasn't working nearly as hard as her sister was.

"One more time, Cris," she urged. "Just one more time. Third time's the charm, you know that. C'mon, honey, you can do this."

Exhaustion was etched into Cris's thin, classic features. "I…don't…know Andy. I'm so…tired," Cris gasped. "I don't…think…I…can…do…this."

Raising her eyes, Andy exchanged looks with Shane. He was beginning to seem really worried.

She sure hoped there was nothing unusual in what her sister was going through. Because what did she really honestly know?

And where was Logan with Dorothy?

"Yes, you can," she insisted. "Don't make a liar out of me, Cris. You're the strong sister, the heroic one, remember?" She tried to will her strength to her sister. "You can't give up now. If you fold, you know Alex will buckle under the pain. Do this for Alex," she coaxed. "Just one more time, Cris. One more big push. Bring that baby home."

"Okay…one more…time," Cris gasped.

With Shane propping her up and supporting her back, Cris dragged in a huge breath and used it to help her bear down.

She gave it all she had.

Watching, Shane's eyes became huge when the baby began to emerge. There was disbelief in his voice as he asked Andy, "Is that—?"

"You bet it is," Andy answered excitedly. "It's happening, Cris. You're making it happen. Here comes your little bundle of trouble!" she announced, never taking her eyes off the baby as more and more of the tiny human being came into view.

Supporting the baby's head, Andy did

what she could to help ease it out into the world.

"The head's out, Cris. Now the shoulders and you're both home free. One more push, one more big push," she urged over and over.

Her sister looked beyond exhausted, closing her eyes and stifling a guttural cry.

"Done!" Andy cried, drawing the newest addition to their family completely out. "You've got a girl, Cris. A beautiful, perfect little girl." Exhilarated, Andy did a quick inventory of the newborn. "She's got everything she's supposed to and nothing that she's not supposed to," she told them.

Gazing down at the baby she was holding in her arms, Andy realized she still had things to take care of. "I need a knife or scissors, rubbing alcohol, something to clamp the cord with…maybe a big paperclip?…and a blanket or a clean sheet to wrap around your little princess," she told Shane.

Gently laying Cris back on the pillow, Shane slipped out from behind his wife. He was about to hunt for the things Andy requested, but someone else beat him to the punch.

"Right away," Dorothy said.

Cradling this brand-new life against her own breast, Andy looked up to see that Logan had finally returned with the house-keeper, who went to retrieve everything they needed.

Andy did the honors and, after cutting the umbilical cord, clamped the end.

"Here, Miss Andy, give that pretty little child to me so I can clean her up properly. Once I've got her tucked into her blanket, I'll introduce this princess to her parents."

Relieved and incredibly happy, Shane slipped his arms around his wife and just held her. "We do pretty great work to-gether," he told her, watching his daugh-ter being cleaned up.

Too tired to speak, Cris smiled at him and held on to his hand.

Andy shifted so that she was on Cris's other side. "Are you all right?" she wanted to know.

Cris nodded, then whispered, "Very all right." Her mouth curving just a fraction more, she mouthed "thank you" to her sister.

"Don't mention it," Andy murmured, struggling to her feet.

Andy had spent the past twenty minutes in a singularly uncomfortable crouch to give Cris a sense of space and not crowd her.

There was a sudden cramp in her calf as she tried to stand and Andy almost sank down again.

Logan grabbed her hand and drew her up.

"Thanks." She took a deep breath to steady her frayed nerves. "I'd given up on you."

"Dorothy wasn't the easiest person to find," he told her. "Especially with so many bodies milling around. When I got back to the common room, your father and Dorothy were trying to get your other sister's wedding back on track."

"Stevi. I forgot all about Stevi," Andy cried, flustered. How could she forget about Stevi? This was supposed to be her big day.

Logan laughed. "Under the circumstances, I think she'd understand. Besides, from what I saw, she and Mike are wrapped around each other. No offense but I don't think she even noticed you were missing."

"None taken—and I hope you're right," Andy added.

Meanwhile, Logan gave her the once-over. "I think your outfit might be ruined."

Andy looked down at the dress she'd put on just before the wedding.

She shrugged. "Dirty clothes are the least of my worries," she told him. Something else had been preying on her mind these past few minutes. "When you were searching for Dorothy, did you happen to see Alex anywhere?"

Shane overheard her question and quietly laughed. "Delivering one baby isn't enough for you?" he asked. "You're looking to deliver two?"

"Delivering one is *more* that enough—Daddy," Andy assured her brother-in-law. "Well, if you two don't need me anymore, I'm going to change into something else." But before leaving, she patted her sister's arm. "You did good, Cris. Ricky is going to just love his new baby sister."

After kissing Cris's cheek and giving Shane a hug, Andy left the room.

"Is this what it's like?" Logan asked, falling into step beside her as she hurried back into the corridor, away from Cris and Shane's suite.

"Is this what what's like?" she asked, her mind going in several different directions at once.

"Having a family," Logan said. "Is it always nonstop activity like this?"

This was, she thought, family life at its most chaotic.

"It is if two of the siblings are pregnant and another one is getting married. Family isn't something that you take out of a box once in a while, or notice around the holidays. Belonging to a family is a twenty-four/seven sort of deal. Sometimes you just want to run away, screaming, because it makes you so crazy. But most of the time, you're happy knowing that there's always someone who has your back, who cares if you're happy or sad."

He didn't look 100 percent convinced. "If you ask me, it seems hectic and demanding."

"It is hectic and demanding," she agreed. "But I've never known any other way and I'm pretty sure that the silence, if I wasn't part of a family, would probably kill me."

"That's a little dramatic," he commented.

He found her smile exceedingly compelling. Logan felt as if he was being reeled in.

"Maybe," she acknowledged. "But then, so am I."

He was about to remark on that when he realized that she'd stopped walking and he hadn't. Turning around he looked at her. "What?"

She nodded toward the door behind her. "This is my room."

"Oh. I guess you want to change, then."

"That was the idea," Andy pointed out. With that, still smiling, she went inside her room and closed the door behind her.

She'd been doing that a lot these past couple of days, Andy realized. Smiling at Logan. Giving the man points when all he was doing was behaving like a normal human being—one who didn't have an ax to grind or an inn to steal out from under them.

Just because he behaved like a normal person shouldn't make her view him as somebody extraordinary. Normal was supposed to be…well…normal.

Leaving her stained dress in a heap on the floor, Andy quickly pulled on a pair of jeans and a dark blue pullover. Her hair was in her way so she clipped it back and swiftly fashioned it into a French twist.

Stepping into a pair of mules, she was ready, eager to go searching for Alex. If nothing else, she wanted to let Alex know that Cris had beaten her to the punch and given birth to a daughter.

She threw open her door again and gasped as, in her enthusiasm to find Alex, she walked smack into Logan.

It took her a second to regain control over herself. "What are you doing here?" Andy wanted to know, backing up.

"Standing. Apparently getting run into," Logan added for good measure. "You do realize that you came out of there as if someone had shot you out of a cannon, don't you?"

"Come on," she said, hauling him forward by the arm. "Let's check on Alex."

"You really are like a mother hen, aren't you?" Logan said, letting her drag him down the hall.

"Not exactly a description I'd cherish, but if you say so." She peeked sideways at him. "I thought you'd be back to the reception."

"I decided to wait for you—in case you needed something."

What void could this man possibly fill for her—other than the obvious? She knew what she needed. Yet she doubted Logan was prepared to go back to his client and convince the California government to find another property for their grand development plan.

Just what was this man's game, anyway? Did he think if he was nice enough to her, she'd just forget about what he was poised to do—separate her family and her from the only place they had ever called home?

Fat chance. Good-looking, sexy guy or

not, she wasn't about to walk away from this one without one long, dragged-out fight, Andy vowed.

"I do know how to get around here, you know," she told him, thinking he was offering to guide her back to reception.

"Okay, then you can guide me back. I'm completely turned around," Logan told her cheerfully. "I don't have the best sense of direction and I've already been turned around a few times in this place."

She was already headed toward the wedding reception, but that made her slow up. She hadn't seen that one coming. His admission, so completely against the male code, surprised her.

"Most men don't admit to not being able to find their way around," she told him.

He appeared unfazed by that little bulletin. "I'm not most men."

Andy looked at him for a long moment. She could feel something stirring in her. Oh great. She was attracted to someone who could still very well turn out to be the enemy to the end.

She needed to get a grip.

"So I've gathered," she replied, more to herself than to him. "By the way, thanks for going with me to the basement and getting the generator going."

"Nothing to thank me for. I wasn't too keen on spending my stay here groping around in the dark."

"Well, thank you anyway," she said stiffly.

Andy spotted her father just then, as well as her nephew. Relieved, she immediately headed straight for them.

Her father saw her before she even reached him and the boy. "How is Cris?" he wanted to know.

"Is my mom okay?" Ricky asked at the same time.

"She's doing just fine, men," she assured the two of them. "Oh, by the way, Dad, you have a granddaughter," she added, her eyes shining.

She could see that the news caught her father by surprise.

"She had the baby?" Richard cried.

Andy nodded. "Just a few minutes ago.

You're a big brother now, Ricky," she told her nephew, crouching down to his level.

"Can I go see the baby? Can I?" he begged, grabbing her by the hand and jumping up and down.

"Well, I don't see why not. Grandpa will take you to her," she replied. "But your mom's kind of tired out, so don't stay too long, okay?"

"Okay!" Ricky said, bobbing his head up and down.

Richard took his grandson's hand in his. "Come on, boy, let's go see your little sister and your mom and dad." He didn't have to say it twice.

"Moves fairly fast for an old…er gentleman," Logan observed.

"Nice save," Andy commented, amused.

"Thanks." They were sharing a moment, he realized.

Scanning the immediate area for her sister, Andy paused for a moment and looked at him. "You really can be a nice person when you want to be, can't you?"

The man kept surprising her like that—

was that to get her to lower her guard? Or were she and her family getting to him?

Logan was cavalier in his response. "Maybe you bring it out of me."

"Ah, if only." Andy sighed.

If what he said was true, she could convince him to help her put an end to the state's demands. But until he told her otherwise, the man who had been with her for what felt like most of the day could turn back into the enemy in a blink of an eye.

All she could do was focus on the positive things. And there were positives.

Her father looked better tonight than he'd looked in a month, Stevi got her wish and was married at the inn and Cris had a beautiful baby girl to round out her family.

She couldn't get greedy, Andy told herself. She'd already been on the receiving end of so much. To pray for more might be rocking the boat.

Still, she couldn't help herself. She wanted it all to resolve itself into a near fairy-tale ending.

"There she is," Logan announced. He pointed some distance behind her.

"Who?" she asked.

"Aren't you trying to find Alex?" he replied.

Blinking, she nooded…trying to ignore the ringing in her ears that Logan seemed to be causing. Andy looked around. "Where?"

"Over there." Using his hands, he physically turned her head to the exact line of vision. "In a chair. She's the one with Wyatt hovering over her."

Andy finally saw what Logan had spotted. Wyatt had his back toward them. She recognized her brother-in-law's stance, but as far as she could see, there was no way that Logan could have seen the man's face to identify him. Apparently Logan came with hidden talents.

Still, curiosity prompted her to ask, "How can you possibly tell it's Wyatt?"

"Easy. He's got the same set to his shoulders that Shane had when he was standing next to Cris during labor."

Could he actually be that discerning when he was looking at someone? She supposed lawyers were trained to read body language and recognize clues like that.

"That's a pretty sharp eye you have there," she said cautiously.

"It comes in handy when I'm trying to read a jury," he said, confirming her suspicion.

And just like that, the threat that Logan MacArthur represented stole her breath away.

Not yet, she schooled herself, reluctant to surrender even an extra minute of this reprieve of thinking of Logan as a lawyer. She still had until dawn the next day. A lot could happen before dawn.

Somehow, she had to get through to him.

But that was just going to have to wait, she told herself, until after the wedding reception concluded and the bride and groom left on their honeymoon. And it was going to have to wait until Cris was settled in with her brand-new baby.

Except that if she waited until the rain stopped and Stevi and Mike were able to leave for their honeymoon...that meant

Logan would be leaving, too, and her time would be up.

She was so confused.

With Logan right behind her, Andy made a beeline for where her oldest sister was sitting.

The closer she came to Alex, the paler her sister seemed.

Wyatt moved to one side as she approached.

"Alex," Andy began very quietly, "are you all right?"

"No," Alex replied in a very still, very controlled voice.

"What's wrong?" Andy took her hand and looked into Alex's eyes.

For the very first time that she could ever recall, Andy saw fear there.

"My water broke."

CHAPTER SEVENTEEN

OH NO, NOT AGAIN.

Andy's head throbbed.

This couldn't be happening twice in such a short space of time. The fact that truth was stranger than fiction didn't sway her from her position.

This just *couldn't* be happening and that was the end of it.

"Are you sure, Alex?" Andy asked, bending down to be at eye level with Alex. "Maybe, in all the excitement, what with the wedding, the power outage, the storm and everything else that's going on right now, you just *think* your water broke. Maybe it's just the baby pressing on your bladder, causing, you know, an accident," she suggested gently.

Her sister moved her head emphatically from side to side. Biting down on her lower lip as she struggled with the latest contraction, it took Alex a moment before she was able to breathlessly squeeze her words out.

"I know the difference, Andy. This isn't an accident." She indicated the dampness beneath her. "This is my water breaking."

Alex was still sitting on the chair but now, Andy noticed, her sister was gripping either side of the chair *hard*, her knuckles turning almost white from the force she was expending.

"Are you having a contraction right now?" Andy asked her, vainly hoping for a negative answer. But Alex nodded her head, her eyes never leaving Andy's.

"The baby's coming," Wyatt said needlessly. Judging by his tone, Andy realized that the man was trying very hard not to panic, for Alex's sake. "We need to do something."

"And Alex is doing it." Rising to her feet, she stepped back. "We need to get her into your room—or at least out of here," she told Wyatt. "I don't think Alex is quite up to being the entertainment portion of Stevi's wedding."

Alex emitted a high-pitched sound in

protest of the very idea Andy had mentioned.

"Put your arms around my neck, Alex," Wyatt coaxed, preparing to lift her.

Breathing quickly to keep the contraction at bay, Alex pointed out, "That's how this started in the first place."

Wyatt brushed his lips against hers. "It started because you're so irresistible," he corrected her. Slipping his arm beneath her legs, he lifted Alex from her chair, then looked over his shoulder toward Andy. "Where to?"

"If you're up to carrying her to your room, then that would be best."

"What do you mean, 'up to'? I'm not that heavy," Alex protested.

"Nice to know you're still feisty," Wyatt commented. "Our room it is." He began walking in that direction. "The doctor's not going to be able to get here in time to help Alex, is he?" Wyatt asked uneasily.

In time suggested that the man would eventually be able to reach the inn and as of yet, that just wasn't possible.

"He's not going to get here at all," Andy

said as she quickly walked ahead of them. "The last I checked, even phone calls weren't going through. But that doesn't mean we can't keep trying."

Andy turned toward the man who was bringing up the rear. "Logan, when we reach the room, can you use the landline to try to get a call through to the doctor?"

She could recite the doctor's phone number from memory at this point.

"Who knows? We might get lucky and get through," she said for Alex's benefit.

"Even if I get through, that still doesn't mean that he'll be able to get here," Logan reminded her, thinking of his own frustrating situation.

"Think positive," Andy instructed him. She turned her attention to Alex. "The good news is that yours isn't the first baby I've delivered tonight so I'm not quite the novice you think I am."

"You delivered a baby?" Alex cried, stunned. "Whose baby?"

The question came out more like a gasp than an actual question as a contraction ripped through her, bringing with it a huge wall of pain that, mercifully, was gone within the next ten seconds.

Her sister's water had only just broken. How was Alex in hard labor this fast?

This was getting bad, Alex thought nervously. She wasn't ready for this.

"Whose do you think?" Andy asked her with a wide grin.

There was only one choice available to her. "Cris? Cris had her baby?" Alex cried just as they reached the room.

Andy quickly opened the door for them, then stood back next to Logan, allowing Wyatt—and Alex—in first.

Heading straight for their queen-size bed, he gently laid his wife down.

"Cris had her baby," Andy confirmed.

Alex looked as if she wanted to jump up and hurry to her sister. Instead, Wyatt very gently pushed her shoulder until she sank back down against the bed.

"What did she have? Boy? Girl?" Alex asked.

Andy grinned. "Those are the two choices," she agreed.

Alex turned toward her husband. "Hit her, Wyatt. I can't reach her."

"Can't, honey. Andy's a girl and I can't hit a girl," Wyatt told her. Positioning himself next to her on the left side of the bed, he took Alex's hand in his. He no sooner did that than she went rigid. Wyatt paled. "Andy, what's wrong with her?" he asked nervously.

"Off the top of my head, I'd say Alex was in labor and in pain," she answered.

She saw that her sister was doing her very best not to scream. She had a feeling that was because Cris hadn't screamed during her first delivery. For some reason, that had set the bar for Alex, but it wasn't realistic.

"Alex, it's okay," Andy coaxed. "You can scream if it helps."

"*Nothing* will help unless you get this baby out of meee!"

Grabbing Wyatt's hand, Alex held on for dear life, channeling her pain through her hand and toward her husband, cutting off the circulation to his fingers.

"Wow, I had no idea you had that kind

of a grip," he marveled. Alex was still clutching him very tightly. She had all but brought him to his knees as she hung on to him.

"I got him!" Logan suddenly cried.

Busy preparing Alex, Andy had almost forgotten about the other man. She looked at him over her shoulder. "Got who?"

"The doctor." He held up the phone.

How could she have forgotten that she told him to keep trying to reach the doctor? Andy berated herself. "Can he come? Tell him that Alex's water broke," she told Logan as she watched her sister make divots in her mattress. "And she went into labor really fast."

Wyatt relayed the message to the doctor, then listened to his response. His eyes meeting Andy's, Logan shook his head.

"The freeway is still flooded. He's already tried to get to Ladera twice—to check on Richard—but with no luck."

"Keep him on the line," Andy said. "I am not doing this by myself—again—oh, and tell him about Cris, would you please? That she and her baby girl are fine. I think…I mean, I'm sure they are."

She looked from Wyatt to Alex and then back at Logan. "He absolutely can't get here?"

Logan shook his head, holding his hand over the receiver.

Something told Andy that she was going to need all the help she could get, despite her vast experience at delivering babies, and since it wasn't easy reaching anyone by phone—landline or cell—she intended to keep this line of communication open as long as she could. Just in case.

A strong feeling of déjà vu washed over her as she said, "Wyatt, get on the bed behind Alex. I'm going to need you to prop her up and support her shoulders so she can bear down and push when I tell her to. Ready?" she asked, glancing up at Wyatt.

"As much as I'll ever be," her brother-in-law responded.

When she'd checked just now, her oldest sister appeared to be even more dilated than Cris had been at the outset. That was a good thing.

"Okay, Alex, when I say push, I want you to push as hard as you can. Got that?"

"I'm not stupid," Alex answered. "Got it."

Her sister already sounded exhausted, Andy thought uneasily. Bracing herself and offering up a little prayer that all went well, Andy ordered Alex to push.

She watched as Alex's face turned pink, then red then close to a bright shade of purple. A guttural cry ripped out of her throat as Alex focused every fiber of her being on pushing the baby out.

But nothing happened, and when Andy examined her again, she saw that there hadn't been even an infinitesimal amount of progress.

An all but paralyzing thought occurred to Andy and she carefully felt around the infant's shape within Alex's belly.

"Hold the phone up to my ear," she told Logan.

Taking care to keep his eyes averted from Alex, Logan did exactly as Andy requested.

"I think the baby's breech," Andy told the doctor.

Andy sounded calm as she made the statement, but her heart was banging inside her chest like a drum. Listening very closely to every word the doctor told her, Andy felt almost a numbness spread over her.

"Okay, I think I can do that," she said, only because she knew she had to make Alex believe that everything was under control and would turn out all right. Andy felt as if she was sweating bullets. "Doc, please, I need you to stay on the phone with me until this is over. I think Alex will feel a lot better about it, too."

"Sure," said the voice in her ear. "It's not like I can go anywhere to render assistance."

"Great." Andy's mind was racing around a mile a minute. She raised her eyes to her sister's and braced herself. "Alex, I have to turn the baby so he or she can come out. This isn't going to be pleasant for either one of us," she warned.

"Just...do...it!" Alex cried through

clenched teeth. There were tears in her eyes, generated by the pain she was experiencing. But she looked determined to get through this.

As gently as possible, working on the outside as well as switching off and moving the baby from within, Andy focused on slowly turning the infant the necessary forty-five degrees to achieve a normal birth process.

Alex was grabbing handfuls of her bedclothes, bunching them up, screams breaking free when she wasn't able to hold them back.

Ninety seconds later, she all but collapsed onto the bed again as Alex cried, "Done. It's done. The baby's in the right position." Taking a deep breath to fortify herself, sweating profusely, Andy told her sister to brace herself.

After all was said and done, it took an additional endless hour, but finally, Alex and Wyatt's first offspring, a very lusty-voiced baby girl, made her appearance just three minutes before midnight.

Logan had held the cell phone up to

her ear the entire time without a word of complaint, even when his forearm began cramping up.

She couldn't have done it alone and she was grateful for the help as well as being endlessly grateful that it was all over.

Andy felt as if she could just collapse in a heap where she was.

Smiling weakly at the duo as they stared wordlessly at the baby in Alex's arms, she declared in a quiet voice, "Congratulations."

Wyatt momentarily left his post by Alex's side and embraced Andy in a heartfelt bear-hug. "Thank you," he said with so much feeling, it oozed out of the words.

As she started to walk out of the room, her knees nearly buckled. Never far away from her, Logan was quick to catch Andy to keep her from falling.

For the second time.

At least there were no more babies to deliver tonight.

Andy found herself looking up at him. "Thanks."

"Can you walk?" he asked as he helped

to guide her out of the room, giving the brand-new parents some privacy with their newborn.

"Barely," Andy acknowledged. "I think my legs fell asleep." She blew out a long, cleansing breath, just as she had been instructing her sisters to do at various stages of their deliveries. "I sure hope nobody else is pregnant here tonight. With my luck, they'll go into labor the minute they look at me."

Logan laughed. "This was a pretty amazing day."

"And weird," Andy threw in. "Very weird. Who would have ever thought my sisters would deliver on the same day, especially since their due dates were about two weeks apart?"

"I guess the babies didn't want to miss out on all the excitement of the wedding," he said.

She smiled weakly. "I guess."

He left his arm around her, carefully guiding her out into the corridor. He found he rather liked the idea of watching over her, even though he'd probably never met another woman quite as self-sufficient, as capable as Andrea Roman.

"Your sisters were lucky you were around," he told her. Reviewing the events of the day in his mind, he ventured a comment. "It wasn't just the day that was pretty amazing—you were pretty amazing tonight, did I tell you that?"

"No, but you can if you like," she said with an encouraging, albeit exhausted smile.

Ordinarily, compliments made her awkward, but right now, hearing him say this, made her feel very warm and contented.

"Well, if we're talking about what I'd like…" Logan's voice drifted off for a moment as he stopped walking and faced her.

Andy's heart went into double-time.

"Yes?" she whispered, her eyes never leaving his.

"What I'd like to do is this," Logan said simply—a moment before he lowered his mouth to hers and kissed her.

As exhausted as she was, Andy could feel her insides start spinning.

The force was such that her breath was stolen away.

Trying to pull back—mentally if not physically—Andy struggled to pull herself together.

It was at that moment she realized that she had threaded her arms around the back of Logan's neck and, rather than call a stop to it, had caused the kiss to continue on—until she was utterly numb.

And then, just like that, Logan drew his mouth away from hers.

"But I won't because you might just have my head if I kissed you," Logan told her. His eyes were dancing with amusement.

She could feel the smile building in her, slipping over her lips, working its way into her eyes.

"Maybe I won't. This one time, I'll leave your head intact," she said.

Logan left his arms around her. Somehow it felt right holding her this way. Because everyone seemed to be either still at the reception in the common room or in their own rooms for the night, so they had this small alcove in the corridor to themselves. And Logan planned to fully enjoy it.

"You pulled together a wedding, rescued your sister's ceremony from becoming a possible disaster and then helped your other two sisters give birth," he marveled. "What do you do for an encore, leap tall buildings in a single bound or do you bend steel in your bare hands?"

"How about just collapsing in a heap on the floor? Because I could absolutely manage to do that," she told him.

The way she felt, she could very easily follow through on that action.

"Well, in that case, what do you say that I just get you to your room before you and the floor become better acquainted?" Logan suggested.

"Sounds like a plan."

The last thing she wanted was to make good on that image. God knew she could definitely sleep, possibly even while she was standing up.

But there was also an excitement throbbing inside her.

Her time was very limited.

Because, come the dawn, they—she and Logan—were going to have to retreat to their separate corners on opposite sides of the glaring issue she was doing her very best to ignore for now: selling the inn.

Whether by choice—or at gunpoint—if a miracle didn't intervene, her father was going to be required to sell or hand over the deed to the family inn to an outsider who in turn would allow the state's bulldozers to ravage the inn as well as the land it was sitting on.

She didn't want to think about it. And kissing Logan was one very good way to get herself not to think about it. Or about anything else for that matter.

The man had a very lethal mouth.

CHAPTER EIGHTEEN

THE NEXT MOMENT, Andy forced herself to pull away from Logan's kiss.

Nothing would get resolved that way.

After the day she had put in, part of her felt that she should just say good-night, crawl into her bed and attempt to recharge her batteries as much as possible—especially since it was going to be up to her to cover as many bases as she could tomorrow. This was *not* the time to get into a potential discussion—or worse, an argument—with the man who, for whatever reason, had stepped up when she needed him today.

But she also knew that the question buzzing around in her head needed answering and if she didn't at least ask she wasn't going to get any decent sleep tonight.

"What are they going to do with it?"

She could see that she had caught him completely off guard. "The state. What is it that they want to do with the land the inn is standing on?"

Had she asked last week, or even three days ago, he would have answered matter-of-factly without a second's hesitation. He had been immersed in the details, but removed from the reality of the issue.

He wasn't removed any longer. These past three days had pulled him in and opened his eyes so that he could now see it all from Richard Roman's viewpoint.

The answer to her question made him uncomfortable. It made perfect sense last month, but not now, not after he had gotten to know her and her family. Not after he had become a guest at the inn that was marked for destruction.

"The plans are to build a giant shopping mall," he told her quietly.

"A giant shopping mall," Andy repeated. She didn't know whether she felt more horrified or insulted by the suggestion. "And this is an improvement over the inn how?" she wanted to know. How could anyone,

anyone choose a mall over a picturesque inn that had a history with the community?

"It's a matter of revenue," he explained. And for the first time in his life, he found the idea of money winning out over character rather off-putting. "A mall would bring in more taxable income than the inn does."

She'd assumed something like that, but hearing it in so many words seemed even more offensive. "So it all boils down to money."

"Everything boils down to money," Logan replied.

That had been an edict he had pretty much believed all his life. But what he had witnessed here at the inn these past couple of days had him questioning the principles that had shaped so much of who he was.

"No, it doesn't," Andy insisted. "That's not how my family sees it. And that's not how the guests who come here see it. A lot of good things happen here at Ladera by the Sea, things you *can't* put a price tag on."

He really didn't want to have this conversation now and tried his best to ease his way out of it. "I get the fact that you're attached to this place, Andy—"

"It's not a place, it's our life," she told him fiercely.

He tried to get her to focus on the positive—a side that wouldn't have occurred to him before he'd been forced to stay with these people, forced to join in and see life from Andy's side.

"You and your family will find another inn to run. A better, more modern one."

She looked at him, shaking her head. He was missing the point.

"It's not about new and shiny, Logan. It's about traditions and heritage."

Andy realized that she could go on arguing this point all night and she could still fail to win him over. "Wait, I've got something for you."

The next moment, Andy disappeared into her room, leaving Logan to stand idly before her door, waiting. He finally put his hand on the doorknob, about to go into her room when the door opened again.

Andy looked very pleased with herself. She was holding a hardback book in her hands. A book she obviously wanted him to read.

"Here," she declared, thrusting it at him. When he gazed at her quizzically, she told him, "Your assignment is to read this."

"Now?" he asked.

"You can start it now, finish it tomorrow. The weather report is for more rain, and as you pointed out there's no TV in your room so think of this as being educational diversion."

Curious now, Logan turned the book around and looked at it for the first time. There was a photograph on the cover that had to have been taken by the same type of camera that had been used to photograph generals in the Civil War.

The photograph, in shades of brown, depicted the inn as it had originally appeared when Ruth Roman began taking in guests.

For a second, all he could do was stare at it. "Wait, is this whole book about the inn?" he asked.

She nodded. The book had been out for a year and was still selling well from what she'd heard. They were all very proud of it—and of Wyatt, who had always been more of a big brother to her and her sisters. All except for Alex, of course.

"It is," she confirmed. "Wyatt's father, Dan Taylor, was my Dad's best friend. He was an investigative journalist who used to spend his summers here with Wyatt. As a gift to my dad, Uncle Dan decided to write Ladera by the Sea's history."

"Uncle?" Logan questioned.

"An honorary title," she explained. "When Uncle Dan died before he could see the project through, Wyatt took over and finished it. The book is all about the inn's history, about the people who stayed here. Regular people like Ms. Carlyle, and famous people like Clark Gable and Spencer Tracy, but also soldiers, lost souls who needed a temporary place to stay—"

"Like me," he said, thinking that was her point in getting him to read the book.

Andy smiled. "Like you," she agreed. "Maybe if you read Wyatt's book, you'll understand why this place is so important and so very special to us—as well as to the people in the area."

He already realized that.

But there wasn't anything he could do about it. Even if he chose to step down and not represent the state, another lawyer would be put in his place. Eminent domain was a force to be reckoned with and almost impossible to dismiss or get around.

Logan looked down at the book she'd given him. Maybe there was something useful in its pages. It couldn't hurt to check.

"I'll read it," he told her, but he had no intention of raising her hopes unless he could find something to work with. "But even if it makes me understand where you're coming from, that still doesn't change the fact that the state can invoke eminent domain if it has to and seize the land right out from under you."

She pushed the book a little closer to Logan's chest. "Just read it," she urged. There had to be something there that would sway him and possibly the state.

Very lightly, Andy brushed her lips over his. "See you in the morning," she said, "if we don't all float away in the middle of the night."

With that, she slipped into her room and closed her door.

Logan stood there for more than a minute, thinking of the last few frantic hours he'd spent in her company. With a sigh, he glanced at the book's cover again. Life had to have been a great deal more peaceful then, he couldn't help thinking.

With that, Logan shrugged to himself. If nothing else, maybe the book would help put him to sleep. Right now, he felt far too agitated.

LOGAN STAYED UP a good part of the night, reading. Rather than the dry, pedantic book he was expecting, he found it engaging. It managed to emulate the warm, laid-back and friendly atmosphere he'd discovered at the inn. Moreover, the book subtly drew him into the various stories that were detailed in the book's pages.

Somewhere after two o'clock, Logan fell asleep, with the book spread-eagled across his chest.

Logan found himself dreaming about the inn. But it wasn't the one he had become familiar with these past few days. The inn in his dreams was more like the version that was depicted on the cover of the book.

It was a great deal smaller in his dream than the one he had walked through earlier today. This was the inn that had been standing when Ruth Roman changed it from a family home to a family source of income.

As his dream continued, the inn kept changing, mirroring the various renovations and additions that had taken place over the years. In his book, Wyatt had included photographs depicting each stage of the subtle evolution.

His subconscious had absorbed it all.

And as Logan drifted from room to room in his dream, he became aware of boisterous laughter and raised men's voices. He sensed rather than saw a poker game being played in what eventually was to become the common room.

The participants, all men except for one very striking woman at the table—a woman who looked a great deal like Andy—were dressed in soldier's uniforms.

But the uniforms belonged to a different era. They appeared to predate World War I.

The most boisterous of the crew was a big-boned, mustached man wearing a monocle and smoking a cigar.

Logan woke with a start, bolting upright in bed. He quickly scanned the room, fully expecting to find the soldiers seated around the table, still playing poker.

Layer by layer, the truth became evident to him. What had woken him up was not the group of men laughing and telling tall tales of heroism, but the wind. It was howling and rattling his window like someone trying to break in.

Taking a deep breath, Logan rubbed his face, trying to focus his mind.

It had been a dream, vivid, but just a dream. What he'd been reading just took hold of his imagination when he'd fallen asleep.

It had felt so real—but it wasn't.

Logan glanced at his watch. It was almost eight o'clock. It was so dark outside—wasn't the rain *ever* going to stop?—that it could have just as easily been eight at night.

Seeking solace in the routine, Logan took a quick shower and shaved. Less than half an hour after he'd woken up from his rather unique dream—an oddity in itself since he seldom dreamed—Logan was venturing downstairs.

Walking through the dining room, he was surprised to find several of the inn's guests seated at tables. And they were having breakfast. Cris had just given birth the night before.

How hearty were these Roman women, anyway? he caught himself wondering.

Logan walked into the kitchen. He saw a Roman making several meals on the industrial stove, but not the one he'd expected to find. Andy, not Cris, was manning several frying pans.

Nodding at Jorge, Logan stood observing Andy for a moment before voicing his surprise. "You cook?"

She turned and looked at him as if she'd been expecting him to turn up at her elbow right about now.

"Cris is recuperating. Someone has to feed the inn's guests. After all, it *is* called a bed and breakfast," she reminded him. "And it's not like I don't have help," she pointed out, nodding at Jorge. She gave him a quirky smile as she continued preparing several meals at the same time. "So, what'll it be?"

"Just coffee."

She shot him a reproving look. "You need more than that. Haven't you heard? Breakfast is the most important meal of the day. You don't eat a good breakfast, the rest of your day is shot."

He was familiar with the philosophy though he had never taken it to heart. However, in the interest of peace, he said, "Okay, I'll have toast."

"And eggs. Sunny-side up. With bacon," Andy decided, voicing his order for him. "Go out and sit in the dining room," she instructed. "Your breakfast will be ready in a few minutes. I'll bring it out to you."

He had learned that arguing with her was futile, so he nodded and went back into the dining room. Besides, he had to admit that he rather liked the idea of having her bring him a breakfast she'd prepared hereself.

Andy was as good as her word. He had no sooner selected a table and sat down than she came out carrying his breakfast on a tray.

"One complimentary breakfast," she announced, setting the plate and a cup of black coffee on the table in front of him.

Logan considered the way she had arranged his meal. The eggs were made to look like eyes with two slices of bacon serving as eyebrows. A third slice of bacon was arranged into a frown.

"It appears my breakfast is scowling at me," he told her. Was this a subtle way to get her feelings across? After all, he was still the embodiment of the threat against their inn.

"That's just your imagination," Andy said, waving away his protest. "Unless you have something to feel guilty about, of course." She paused to flip the piece of bacon that was beneath the eyes, effectively turning the frown into a smile. "There, all better," she declared. The next moment, she hurried back to the kitchen.

AFTER BREAKFAST, LOGAN went back to his room and picked up the book Andy had given him. Something had caught his attention while he was reading last night and he wanted to explore it. But the idea of sitting alone in the suite, reading, didn't really appeal to him. Taking the book with him, he decided to read it in the lobby.

He'd only managed to read another fifteen pages when he heard Andy's voice. Glancing up, he saw that she was now at the reception desk. This time she was filling in for Alex, just as she had for Cris earlier.

Leaving a napkin in the book to mark his place, Logan left the comfort of the winged armchair and crossed to the desk.

"I doubt if you're going to have any people checking in with this weather. Or checking out for that matter," he added, looking through the bay window into the ash-gray world. "Unless, for some strange reason, they live in the vicinity, they're in the same boat—no pun intended—as I am."

He leaned in a little closer so that his

voice wouldn't carry to any of the guests who might be passing through the lobby.

"Isn't there anyone else around to cover for your sisters?"

"As you just pointed out, we're not busy so I don't mind. Stevi wanted to cover the desk—she can't boil water so putting her in the kitchen isn't going to help anything." She smiled at the image of Stevi attempting to cook. "She and Mike were supposed to be on the way to their honeymoon. But even if they could reach the airports— which they can't—all planes are temporarily grounded. But they're still on their honeymoon," she said with a wink that Logan found infinitely appealing.

He couldn't help wondering if Andrea Roman had any idea how attractive she was.

Andy saw that he was holding the book about the inn and there was a napkin in it, which meant that he was marking his place—either that, or he was doing it to make her think he was reading it.

Only one way to find out, she decided. "Are you actually reading the book I gave you, or are you just carrying it around, hoping to absorb it by osmosis?"

He laughed shortly. "I was never any good in chemistry. I cut class the day Ms. Fenner taught osmosis, so I'm not all that clear on the concept."

"Ah. So you're reading it?" she asked, nodding toward the book.

"I'm reading it," he confirmed.

"And—?" She was hoping he had something positive to say about the experience, such as that learning the inn's history was opening his eyes.

"And I'm almost three-quarters of the way through it?"

His voice went up, turning his answer into a question to see if he'd given her the information she was looking for. Beyond that, he didn't want to say anything yet, but he was toying with an idea that might get them the results Andy and her family needed.

Andy sighed, shaking her head. "Are you any closer to understanding why this inn means so much to us? What it meant to whole generations of people who came through its doors?"

"I'm getting there. Slowly," was all Logan was willing to say for the time being. He hadn't counted on Andy's impatience.

This was taking too long and they didn't have much time. There had to be something she could do to stop the state from taking the inn, short of chaining herself to its doors.

Maybe she was crazy, hoping to get advice from the enemy. After all, Logan did represent the state in this battle. But this was the only option she had.

"You don't strike me as a slow study," she told Logan.

"Maybe I'm just a firm believer that slow and steady wins the race," he suggested.

"Or maybe you're just stalling, using delay tactics until it's too late for us to do anything about the state's position."

"You really believe that?" he asked.

"I don't know what to believe," she answered. "Except that a few weeks ago, you showed up, threatening to upend life as my family and I knew it. Maybe I'm crazy, thinking you could help."

He looked at her for a long moment. "You want the book back?" he asked, holding it out to her.

"No, I want you to come up with something to help us save the inn. I want you to do the right thing."

"Your definition of the right thing," he pointed out.

"No, the absolute definition of the right thing," she insisted. "The town of Ladera doesn't need a supersize shopping mall."

"Maybe we should ask your father."

"No need. I know his answer. Like I said, it's not about the money."

"Sometimes it's about bowing to the inevitable," he said gently.

"Would you?" Andy asked, watching him intently. "Would you bow to the inevitable if it meant parting with something that had been part of your life, your family's life since forever?"

It was in his best interests to say yes. And he had bowed to the inevitable. He'd parted ways with his parents. If they weren't that "something that had been part of his life since forever," he didn't know what was.

Had she asked the question two weeks ago, he would have replied in the affirmative. But now he wasn't sure anymore. Maybe he'd been wrong to let his parents slip away so easily. Maybe he wished his parents had put up more of a fight to keep him close...

The parameters had gotten blurred and his thinking had seeped outside of the box. Things weren't so black and white anymore. Especially now that he caught himself rooting for the other side.

For Andy's side.

What had she done to him?

"Is everything all right?" Richard Roman asked, coming up to the reception desk. His question wasn't addressed to his daughter. It was meant for the inn's reluctant guest.

"Everything's as fine as it can be in the middle of a monsoon, Dad," Andy replied. "Why aren't you in bed?"

"Because my inn and my daughter need me. You can't be expected to hold down the fort all by yourself," he told Andy. "And the last time I looked, we're three people down, including the honeymooner."

Andy lifted her chin and a defiance that Logan found fascinating lit her eyes. "I'm a Roman, Dad. That means I can hold down the fort with one hand tied behind my back."

Logan's eyes met Richard's. "I bet she can, too." Facing her father, Logan didn't see the way Andy looked at him.

But Richard did.

CHAPTER NINETEEN

THE NEXT MOMENT Richard noticed the book that was tucked under Logan's arm.

It was impossible for him to see it without thinking of his best friend. Dan's real reason for beginning to write the book was to bring his son, Wyatt, and Alex closer. Diagnosed with terminal cancer, Dan had known at the time that he wouldn't live to finish writing it. But that didn't keep the man from putting a happy ending in motion.

"I see you're reading my son-in-law's book on the inn's history." Looking at the young man, Richard made a calculated guess. "Know your enemy?"

"Just trying to get as much input as I can," Logan replied vaguely. "Andy gave it to me last night. She thought it might inspire me to back off. The problem is, even if I walked off the case, the state would only get someone else to represent them in this."

"So it would hurt less if someone we knew forced us to sell the inn instead of someone we didn't?" Richard asked.

The less he said right now, Logan thought, the better. "That was the original idea."

Richard had always been good with people because he was able to read between the lines and hear what wasn't said. "And now? Exactly what is the idea now?" he pressed.

It was obvious the man wasn't about to drop the matter. Debating with himself, Logan decided to let the inn's owner know a little of what he was hoping to find—if there actually was something that would back up what he was thinking.

"You have to understand that when the state—or any government—declares eminent domain, it's pretty much a done deal that they're going to get their way and that the private citizen must concede."

There was something he wasn't saying,

Andy thought. She could hear it in his voice. "But?"

"But?" Richard asked, looking at Andy.

"Out with it. It's a done deal except for what?"

Logan didn't bother hiding the fact that her intuition impressed him. "You're good," he said.

"I'll be better if you answer my question," she replied, trying to harness her impatience. "It's a done deal except for what?"

Logan knew that telling Andy and her father this piece of information would make it obvious that he had changed sides, but the truth was that he had begun changing sides the moment Richard gave him a room when the storm sabotaged his plans.

"If the owners of the property in question can show that it has some sort of real historical significance, the government will rescind the order to expropriate."

"The inn is a hundred and twenty-one years old," Richard reminded him.

Logan shook his head. "The age of the building isn't enough. In order to set it apart, something of historical significance—however minor—has to have taken place here," Logan explained.

Andy tried to recall everything she remembered ever being told about the inn. "Movie stars have stayed here," she volunteered eagerly.

The next moment, Andy began rattling off the names of the celebrities she remembered hearing Ms. Carlyle talk about. Logan greeted each name with the shake of his head. She appeared frustrated, but he couldn't help that.

"That all makes for charming anecdotes, but it's not enough to save the building. Celebrities frequented the Brown Derby all the time and it was still demolished," he told Andy and her father.

Pausing for a moment, he searched for an example to give the pair. "For instance, if they signed the Declaration of Independence here or if Washington rested here before going on to Valley Forge—"

"The inn wasn't even built then," Richard said. If those were the criteria, then the inn was doomed. "It was converted into an inn shortly before the Spanish-American War."

"Wait, there's an old box in the attic," she said eagerly, looking from her father to Logan. "Stevi and I came across it when we were trying to find Mom's wedding dress."

"Go on," her father urged. "What about the box?"

She knew she was clutching at straws, but at least that was better than nothing. "Well, it was practically falling apart when we moved it out of the way. Heavy, too," she added as if that could somehow tip the scales.

"What was in it?" Logan asked.

"I don't know," she said honestly. "It had a lock on it and we were in a hurry. But it had to either be precious—or important to whoever put it there because why bother locking up something that's worthless?"

Logan refrained from saying that she would be surprised at what people locked up. Instead, he told her, "You might have a point there." There was only one way to find out if what was in the box would ultimately give them the evidence they were looking for. "Why don't you show me where it is and maybe we can find a way to open it."

The corners of Andy's mouth curved. He'd just said exactly what she was thinking.

"Dad, would you mind holding down reception while I bring Logan into the attic?"

"Andy, I ran this inn single-handedly when you girls were little. I think I can manage for a few minutes on my own. Go." He waved his daughter and the lawyer away.

"You realize that this may be nothing," Logan cautioned as he and Andy made their way to the utility room, the inn's access point to the attic.

"I know." Still, she couldn't keep from getting her hopes up. Something had to go in their favor, she thought, crossing her fingers. "But then again," she said in a far more positive voice, "it might be exactly what we need to keep the inn from falling into the state's clutches."

"You mean mine, don't you?" he asked.

Andy shook her head. "I've decided not

to think of you as having clutches—at least for now," she qualified.

There was a chain hanging from the ceiling at the rear of the utility room. Reaching for it, Logan pulled hard. The next moment, the drop-down ladder leading into the attic descended. Shifting his position quickly, Logan secured the locks on either side.

Andy went first. Halfway up, she paused to lean over and hit the light switch. The attic was instantly flooded with light.

"The box is over here," she told Logan, leading the way to the corner.

The same area was also filled with a whole collection of empty cartons that, eleven months of the year, housed the Christmas decorations.

Andy started to drag the metal box closer to him. She was clearly struggling with its weight and striving not to give that impression. She was, Logan thought, the last word in stubborn.

Gently he moved her out of the way and brought the box over to the center of the floor where the light was brightest.

Studying it for a moment, he decided that the lock appeared to be the strongest thing about the long, rectangular chest.

"You don't, by any chance, have a drawer full of old keys do you?" It was worth a shot.

"Not to my knowledge. I guess we'll have to call in a locksmith," Andy said, far from happy about having to remain in the dark even longer.

"We could, although I doubt we'd get one to come out any time soon." He nodded toward a small window on the opposite side of the attic. "It's still pouring outside."

She'd gotten so caught up in what might be in the box that she had completely forgotten they were at the mercy of the storm.

Since Logan seemed to have all the answers, she asked, "So what do we do now?"

"Give me a minute."

Logan slowly positioned the box so that the light was shining directly on the lock. Studying it quietly for a moment, he reached into his pocket and pulled something out that Andy couldn't quite make out. From where she sat, it seemed as if he was holding two very thin, long needles or paperclips that had been straightened.

As she watched, Logan inserted one needle into the lock and then inserted the second one halfway in, at an angle.

"What are you doing?" she wanted to know, certain that it couldn't be what it looked like he was doing.

"Trying to open the lock," he replied simply.

That wasn't the answer she expected, so she asked him point-blank, "Are you picking it?"

His eyes focused on his work, he nodded. "With any luck."

Before she could comment on this decidedly unusual skill set—what lawyer knew how to pick locks?—Logan had pulled the lock off.

Stunned, she couldn't just let this go. "Where did you learn how to do that?" she demanded.

"Before my parents wrapped me up and mailed me off to boarding school, they used to lock me in my room. It was a form of punishment if I talked back, or didn't live up to their image of the perfect child or committed any one of a hundred different transgressions. I'm sure they thought it would help give me inner discipline, but I didn't like the idea of being locked up. It made me feel claustrophobic—so I learned how to pick a lock," he said as if it was the most natural course of events.

Logan put his tools back in his pocket. "Never know when it might come in handy." He took a deep breath. "Okay, let's see what's so important."

The lid on the box had rusted into place and it took more than a bit of coaxing—and a lot of strength—before they managed to pry it off.

Inside the metal box were papers. Some had originally been bound together, but the ties had come loose and the binding had become dried out and cracked, leaving the papers exposed. The ink on them had faded, as well.

Carefully sifting through a few of the sheets, Andy looked up at her companion in this trip into the past and said, "These

look like ledgers where the guests registered."

The box was full of them. Getting to his
feet, Logan looked around the attic.

"Where are the rest of them?" he wanted
to know.

"The rest?" Andy echoed.

"Yes, the rest of the ledgers. The inn's
been around for a hundred and twenty-one
years. This is not a hundred and twenty-one
years worth of registrations," he pointed
out.

Andy rose to her feet next to him and
scanned the area slowly. The attic ran the
length of the inn. That was an awful lot of
territory to cover. There were all sorts of
containers in various sizes and shapes.

Andy stated the obvious. "They could be
anywhere in here." If they were going to
look through all of them, they were going
to need help. "Meanwhile, I want to go
through what's in this box."

Logan was already helping himself to a
stack of the papers. A gum wrapper was
stuck between the first couple of pages.

"If you find a candy bar, it's all yours," he told her.

"Always the gentleman."

Curbing her inclination to rifle through the box quickly, she began systematically sorting through the remainder of the pages. There were all sorts of loose papers, some so faded and fragile they fell apart the moment she touched them.

There were also more than a few spiders in the box, making the search less than a desirable experience for her. She wished she'd brought a pair of gloves along.

Too late now.

DIGGING THROUGH THE rusted metal box looked as if it had paid off. At least that was her hopeful impression as she came to the bottom of the pile of papers, when her fingertips came in contact with something square and hard.

Pushing the last of the papers aside, she found herself staring down at what appeared to be a book. One of those books that came with blank pages and was created for the single purpose of storing the uttermost secrets of a person's soul.

In other words, a diary.

"This is her diary, Ruth Roman's diary," she announced excitedly, holding it up. The next moment, Logan had crossed to her, temporarily abandoning the ledger statements he was reviewing.

Opening the diary, she skimmed over a page or two—and frowned.

"What's the matter?" he asked, sitting cross-legged beside her.

"I thought all the ladies from that era were supposed to have excellent handwriting," Andy said.

"They were," Logan replied. At least that was what he'd thought.

"Well, someone should have told Ruth Roman that good handwriting was a prerequisite in keeping notes that might come to the attention of future generations." Looking down at the opened book, she shook her head. This was going to take a long time. "How are you at reading scribbles?"

"Fair to middling," was Logan's response.

Andy held up the diary and turned it around so that he could see the pages. "Less than fair," he amended as he skimmed over the two pages. His frown matched hers after he tried to read the first few lines. It was definitely a challenge.

"That," he told her, frustrated, "is going to take time. A great deal of time."

"We don't have a great deal of time," she reminded him, equally frustrated. "Maybe if we split the labor," she suggested.

"We can't both read the same book at the same time," Logan pointed out, although he had to admit that the idea of perusing the diary while sitting right beside Andy definitely had something to recommend it.

"No," she agreed. "But we can take turns. When one of us starts to go cross-eyed, the other can step in and start reading. And vice versa."

Logan nodded. "Sounds reasonable enough. Do you want to take the first shift, or would you rather give me the diary to start?"

Ruth was her father's ancestor and she had a far more vested interest in finding something pertinent in the diary than Logan did.

"I'll take it," Andy said.

Her answer came as no surprise to him. "I had a hunch," Logan told her. "I'll look around, see if I can locate more mystery boxes containing diaries or maybe find where the other ledgers are stored."

Andy nodded, hardly hearing what he said. She was busy trying to decipher Ruth Roman's terrible handwriting.

LOGAN STRUCK OUT, unable to locate any more ledgers or diaries. While there were neatly labeled, if rather dust-encrusted, boxes, they turned out to be full of clothing belonging to what amounted to several different eras, starting from Ruth Roman's lifetime right up to the recent past.

It was a treasure trove of nostalgia, Andy thought, conducting a quick inventory. But treasure trove or not, ultimately it did their cause no good.

What they needed was a miracle, she reflected wearily. A genuine, bonafide, no-questions-asked miracle.

With a sigh, she put the lid back on the last box she'd opened. Andy was ready to throw in the towel, at least for tonight.

Tonight? She'd been so caught up in what they were doing, she hadn't realized they'd missed lunch and dinner.

She glanced over to where Logan was still seated. How long did it take to finish skimming the last section of a diary, she wondered irritably.

"Logan—"

He raised his hand for her to be quiet as he finished the page he was on.

Shrugging, she made her way to the ladder. "I'm calling it a night," she told him.

Logan looked up. She could see by his expression that he hadn't heard a word she'd said. "I think this might be it," he announced, seeming rather pleased with himself.

Andy paused. She'd heard him, but she was almost afraid to hold out any hope. It was so hard to pick herself up again when her hopes were dashed.

"What might be it?" she asked cautiously.

"Listen to this. *I am completely aware of the fact that he is the hero of San Juan Hill. The men he brought with him, my friends, everyone within the sound of the man's voice are always telling me that, that he's a brave, brave hero. But if Theodore Roosevelt does not either find a way to contain those cigar ashes he is always spilling, or go outside to indulge in that horrible habit of his, I shall not be held responsible or accountable for the mayhem I might visit on his head.*"

Logan closed the diary.

"Are you sure you didn't write that?" he asked.

What was he talking about? He knew that was Ruth Roman's diary. Did he think she'd forged it?

"I didn't," Andy replied with conviction.

He laughed as he handed the diary back to her. "I'm well aware. But it sure sounds like you."

She was about to protest, saying something to the effect that she didn't remotely sound like that at all when what he had read hit her.

Had he actually found the evidence her family needed to retain ownership of the inn?

"Wait a second, Ruth was talking about Teddy Roosevelt, wasn't she?"

Logan grinned. "None other."

"And he was here, at the inn, making her drapes and the surrounding air stink of cigar smoke," Andy said excitedly.

Logan nodded, feeling far more pleased than he should have at this outcome. "So it would seem," he agreed.

She could hardly get herself to believe it. At the very least, she needed to hear him say it. "Isn't that our proof?"

"It most certainly is," Logan answered, then laughed when Andy threw her arms around him. In her unchecked enthusiasm, she wound up knocking him down. Since her arms were around his neck, she went down with him.

CHAPTER TWENTY

THE CORNERS OF Logan's eyes crinkled as he smiled up at her.

"I believe this is what's called a compromising position," he said quietly.

Logan was doing his best not to react to the fact that Andy had landed squarely on top of him—as if they were two halves of the same whole—and that she had allowed herself to remain in this position while she continued hugging him in her gleeful response to his discovery.

He had, in effect, uncovered the miracle she'd been praying for.

"They're going to be angry with you, aren't they?" she realized suddenly as she looked down into his face.

Logan began to shrug and found that he really couldn't with her on top of him. "They'll get over it."

She was savvy enough to know that not

all organizations were forgiving. "And if they don't?"

"Then I'll be in the market for a new firm," he replied calmly. "It wouldn't be the end of the world. Or of an era," he added, bringing up the connection between his possible dilemma and the one she and her family would have had to face had he not found that particular passage in Ruth Roman's diary. "In any event, it wouldn't be anything I couldn't handle."

Suddenly realizing that she was still on top of him, Andy scrambled back into a sitting position. Logan got up as well, sitting next to her.

"And you're sure that this is enough evidence to qualify the inn as a historical landmark?"

Logan nodded, telling her, "Not my first rodeo. Yes, I'm sure."

She wanted to hug him all over again— for more than one reason. But she only gave voice to the first. "You've done it. You've saved the inn. This'll mean the world to everyone, especially my father." Andy beamed at him. "I can't begin to tell you how grateful I am."

He felt good about that, far better than he would have thought. There was something to be said for doing the right thing, even if it came with consequences.

But right now, he wasn't thinking about consequences. He was thinking about the young woman beside him, the one who had caused him to restructure his world. "Well, if you really mean that—"

"Yes?" Andy coaxed, eager to be able to pay him back for becoming her white knight and riding to her rescue.

"Have dinner with me." Logan anticipated her saying that she'd shared a meal with him before, in the inn's dining room. "At a place of my choosing."

"I have a better idea," she told him, her eyes dancing and utterly charming him. "Do you have any plans for Christmas?"

"Other than finding some widows and orphans to rob?" he asked. "No, why?"

Andy had the good grace to blush, embarrassed at the reference. She was going to make that up to him. "Spend Christmas here with us at Ladera. It's only fitting," she insisted, "considering that, thanks to you, we now have something to really celebrate. How about it?"

He pretended to think the matter over. In reality, there was no decision to be made. Besides, there was no way he could say no to that face. It seemed to light up his very world.

"I guess I can free up my calendar," he said.

Logan was kidding, she could tell. Besides, he'd already made it clear he'd had no contact with his parents in years.

She was also fairly certain there was no woman in his life, significant or otherwise. Had there been, she was sure that at some point in these past couple of days Logan would have indicated a desire to get a call through to her. The fact that there was no such concern told her Logan MacArthur was a completely free man in every sense of the word.

And she was glad of it.

"Good," Andy declared with finality, the corners of her mouth quirking into a smile. "Consider your calendar officially filled up again."

THE MOMENT SHE and Logan descended from the attic, Richard was there to corner them.

"Well?" he asked, an underlying note of anxiety in his voice as he looked from his daughter to the lawyer who had come very close to being the inn's undoing. "Did you find anything?"

Logan looked at Andy. It was, he felt, her news to break.

"We found a happy ending," Andy told her father, grinning.

Someone else, Logan thought, might have drawn the moment out, enjoying the spotlight and being the center of attention as well as the bearer of good news. But Andy apparently had no such requirements. It was one of the things he found himself liking about her. One of *many* things.

"For the inn, or for yourselves?" Richard asked, looking between the two of them. There was something going on here. He could see it even if they couldn't.

"Dad!" Andy cried, an interesting shade of pink swiftly weaving its way up along her neck to her cheeks.

"You were in the attic for a long time," her father pointed out.

"There were a lot of papers to go through," she informed her father. She saw a wide, understanding smile take over his face.

"Yes, I know," he replied, still looking at his daughter pointedly.

"You've been living in a historical landmark, Mr. Roman," Logan said, riding to the rescue.

"We have?" Richard asked. "Really?"

"Really," Logan assured him. "It seems that Teddy Roosevelt spent several days here at your inn. Before he became president and fresh off his victory at San Juan Hill."

"And you're sure of this?" Richard asked cautiously, clearly afraid of getting his hopes up.

Logan nodded. "Ruth Roman documented the entire stay in her diary. Seems she wasn't a fan of the occasional cigar the future president liked to indulge in."

Andy couldn't remain silent any longer. "You realize what this means, don't you?"

she asked her father excitedly, catching hold of his arm. Not waiting for him to respond, she supplied the answer to her own question. "The state can't come and take away the inn because that would be destroying a historical landmark."

The words were no sooner out of her mouth than they heard the clatter of a tray hitting the tiled foyer floor. All three of them turned in unison to see a greatly relieved Dorothy exclaim, "Oh, thank heavens!"

Richard smiled at the woman he had rescued so many years ago. "My sentiments exactly, Dorothy."

There was a bottle of champagne he had put away years ago. With Stevi's wedding over, two babies delivered and now this… it was finally time to bring it out, Richard thought.

LOGAN SAT NEXT to Andy in the dining room for Christmas dinner. The rest of her family were seated there, as well. They had taken their places around a table that was actually made up of several tables to accommodate so many.

Besides over a dozen chairs, there were two bassinets added to the mix, one each for the newest members of the Roman family—or dynasty as Wyatt had taken to saying.

For the most part, Logan remained quiet, content to just look around him and take it all in, listening to the various exchanges.

This was the first Christmas in more than two decades that actually felt like Christmas to him, Logan thought. For more years than he cared to count, he had deliberately treated this day like any other day so that the sharp pain of being alone couldn't penetrate the armor he had wrapped around himself.

But this time was different.

This time he was spending Christmas Day with a family. Granted it wasn't his family, but Andy insisted that it was for as long as he might want it to be—possibly even longer, she had qualified.

"Because we owe everything to you," Andy stressed despite his attempts to discount or minimize his part in this. Beneath it all, Andy thought, the so-called hotshot lawyer was a shy man.

He was also a man who came through when it counted. Calls had been placed and paperwork had been filled out and submitted through the proper channels.

It was all merely a formality he had assured Richard. California loved its historical sites, loved the idea of preserving them. The more the better, so the inn was free to go about its business.

"How does it feel being a hero?" Andy asked him a little later that evening, after dinner was officially over and everyone had adjourned to the reception area to open presents beside the giant Christmas tree.

Logan shrugged off the label. "I'm not a hero," he protested.

"You are to them." She indicated clusters of her family sitting on the floor around the tree, as well as Silvio and Dorothy, who were sitting on the sofa. "And to me," Andy said with feeling. "Don't let the last part go to your head."

Logan laughed. "I'm not stupid," he told her, resisting the urge to put his arm around her.

"No, I never thought you were that," she admitted. "Even when I didn't like you."

They were sitting on a sofa, watching everyone else opening their gifts. Andy couldn't remember the last time she had felt this happy.

"Aren't you going to open your present?" Logan asked.

"I did." She pointed to a small pile of boxes on the table.

"I think you missed one," he told her.

Andy glanced back at the neat pile of gifts she'd gotten from her family. They were all unwrapped. "No, I didn't," she said.

"Yes, you did," he maintained.

"Okay," she said, willing to concede the point. "Where is it?"

"Right there." Instead of pointing out a spot beneath the tree the way she'd expected him to, Logan pointed to a branch.

Nestled in the greenery and decorations

was a small package wrapped in shiny silver with a large blue bow on top.

Andy stood and walked over to it. It was so high up she could barely reach it. Standing on her toes, she managed to just barely brush her fingertips against it, knocking it down off its perch.

She caught the box before it had a chance to fall on the floor.

"Where did that come from?" she asked, certain it hadn't been there before.

Logan shrugged innocently as she came back and sat down beside him. "Don't ask me. You're the one who believes in Santa Claus."

"No, I'm the one *sitting* with Santa Claus," she corrected, think of the gift he had given all of them with his discovery in that diary.

Overhearing her, Ricky piped up. "He's not Santa Claus, Aunt Andy."

"He is to us, honey," Cris told her son. She smiled at Logan and for the umpteenth time, murmured, "Thank you."

"Are you planning on sitting there with

that all night or are you going to open it sometime in the near future?" Logan asked.

Andy continued to look down at the box, her heartbeat picking up speed. The rain had finally abated yesterday and for a number of hours, the sun had come out, reminding one and all of the kind of winter's day Southern Californians usually enjoyed.

Logan had disappeared on her for a few hours and she had assumed that he had gone to the post office so the official papers her father had filled out could be sent to Sacramento by registered mail.

She had no idea that he'd made a quick pit stop to shop.

Andy continued looking at the silver wrapping paper from all conceivable angles as her heartbeat continued ratcheting up.

"If you're trying mental telepathy, I don't think it works with inanimate objects," Logan told her.

"Wise guy."

With that, she peeled away the wrapping paper and found herself looking down at a box.

A ring box.

Andy's breath caught in her throat as she glanced at him quizzically before opening it.

And then everything came to a grinding stop. The Earth halted on its axis, all sound faded to the background and there was nothing except for the ring box in her hand and the gleaming ring within it.

This wasn't a good sign, Logan thought. Andy talked all the time and she wasn't talking. Had he made a mistake and misread the signs?

"You don't have to say yes right away," he told her quickly. "It's just something for you to think about. Take all the time you need before giving me an answer."

Andy's mouth had gone dry and she sat there, staring at the ring and watching the lights from the Christmas tree play off its surface. The gleaming multiple colors were getting trapped in the ring before they went on to shoot beams of light that seemed to encircle everything.

"When?" she whispered.

"When?" Logan repeated, at a loss as to what she was asking him. "When what?"

Andy took a breath, determined not to have her voice crack. "When can I say yes? You said not to say yes right away. How long do I have to wait?"

Was she actually agreeing to marry him?

"It's up to you," he finally told Andy. "You can go ahead and give me an answer any time you think you have the right one."

"Yes," Andy whispered.

"What?" he asked, cupping his ear and pretending he hadn't heard her, just so that he could hear her give the answer again.

Instead, what he heard was everyone in the reception area. Andy, her sisters, their husbands, Ricky, Dorothy, even Silvio, all answering him with one voice: *"Yes!"*

It was a word—and an evening—Logan knew he wouldn't soon forget.

And neither would anyone else.

EPILOGUE

THE HILLSIDE SHOWED very little evidence of the deluge that had assaulted the terrain so relentlessly only a few short days ago.

The sun, once again out in full force, had already begun to draw all the available moisture from the land, allowing Richard to make his way down to the small, private family cemetery without fear of slipping and falling the rest of the way.

Had it been otherwise, Andy would have insisted on accompanying him. And though he loved his daughter—loved all of his daughters as well as the men they had brought into the family—he liked being alone for these visits he paid to Amy and Dan.

He liked to feel as if he was really talking to them rather than addressing mere headstones acting as placeholders for the people who had once borne the names written across them.

He appreciated that his daughters were protective of him and cared about his welfare, but some things a man liked to do on his own.

Visiting the family cemetery was one of them.

"Amy, Dan," Richard said, nodding first at his wife's headstone, then at his best friend's.

"That was a terrible spate of weather that hit us, wasn't it? I thought I was going to have to use a canoe to come out to see you. Not to mention that for a while there, it looked as if I was going to have to find a new final *final* resting place for you two as well as for your handful of neighbors," he said, referring to the half dozen or so other graves that the small cemetery contained.

"I suppose you know all about that eleventh hour miracle." Richard laughed to himself as his words echoed back to him. "The two of you probably sent him, didn't you?" he asked. "That would be right up your alley, Dan. Making me twist in the wind a bit before you come through to save the day. Well, among the three of us, I don't care how it was done, so long as it was done.

"Quite an interesting guy, that Logan MacArthur," he said with a smile. "Andy thinks so, too. He gave her a ring, you know. She's the last one to go. All your girls are spoken for, Amy. Husbands and babies, just like we always wanted for them.

"Cris had a girl, right in the middle of that big storm. They've named her Amy, after you, honey. Andy delivered her. Delivered Alex's baby, too. You know Alex, always wanting to be one up on things. She went into labor right after Cris did. By the way, your first grandchild is a girl, Dan. Danielle Roman Taylor. What do you think of that? Wyatt looks so pleased he could bust," Richard said with a laugh.

"Both babies were born right after Stevi's wedding. Andy handled everything, the wedding, the birthing. *Everything.* That's some girl we have there, Amy. Remember when we used to worry because Andy never finished anything she started? We were afraid she'd wind up facing life that way.

"Well, I don't think we have to worry about that anymore. Our girl is something else again. And thanks to her young man, Logan, I'll be coming down here for a very long time. He found a way to make the state back off by having Ladera declared a historical landmark.

"By the way, we're having a big christening party on the first. I thought that might be a nice way to start off the New Year. I wish you two could be there. That would make it even more special," Richard confided.

"I know, I know, I'm a lucky man and I shouldn't get greedy, but I do so miss you two. Especially you, Amy. No offense, Dan," he added. "I know you're both always with me in spirit, but I can't hug a spirit and I miss that, miss just holding you, Amy.

"Even you were good for a bear hug once in a while, Dan." Richard laughed softly to himself again. "I guess I'd better go and fill my empty arms with a baby or two. That should help. I'll give them an extra hug from the two of you," he promised.

"Until the next time," Richard murmured as he turned to go. Looking away from Amy's grave, he thought he felt something pass against his cheek ever so lightly.

Brushing his fingertips along his skin, he smiled to himself.

"I love you, too, Amy," Richard whispered just before he started back up the hill to his beloved Ladera by the Sea.

* * * * *